Left Guard Gilbert

Ralph Henry Barbour

Left Guard Gilbert

Copyright © 2012 by Indo-European Publishing

Contact:
IndoEuropeanPublishing@gmail.com

The present edition is a reproduction of 1916 publication of this work, produced in the current edition with completely new, easy to read format by Indo-European Publishing.

For an authentic reading experience, the Spelling, punctuation, and capitalization have been retained from the original text.

Cover Design by Indo-European Design Team

ISBN: 978-1-60444-618-0

IndoEuropean
Publishing.com
Los Angeles, CA, USA

CONTENTS

CHAPTER I
THE BOY FROM KANSAS

"HOLD up!"

Coach Robey, coatless, vestless, hatless, his old flannel trousers held up as by a miracle with the aid of a leather strap scarcely deserving the name of belt, pushed his way through the first squad players. The Brimfield Head Coach was a wiry, medium-sized man of about thirty, with a deeply-tanned face from which sharp blue eyes looked out under whitish lashes that were a shade lighter than his eyebrows and two shades lighter than his sandy hair. As the afternoon was excessively hot, even for the twenty-first day of September and in proximity to Long Island Sound, Mr. George Robey's countenance was bathed in perspiration and the faded blue silk shirt was plastered to his body.

"That was left half through guard-tackle, wasn't it? Then don't put the ball in your arm, St. Clair. You ought to know better than that. On plays through the line hold it against your stomach with both hands. How long do you think you'd keep that ball in your elbow after you hit the line? Someone would knock it out in about one second! Now try it again and think what you're doing. All right, Carmine. Same play."

The panting and perspiring backs crouched once more, Carmine shrilly called his signals, Thayer and Gafferty plunged against an imaginary foe as Thursby shot the ball back and St. Clair, hugging the pigskin ecstatically with wide-spread fingers, trotted through the hole, stopped, set the ball on the grass and wiped his streaming face with the torn sleeve of a maroon jersey.

"All right," said the coach. "That will do for today. In on the trot, everyone!"

The first squad, exhaling a long, deep sigh of relief as one man, set their faces toward the gymnasium and trotted slowly off, their canvas-clad legs swish-swashing as they met. Coach Robey walked further down the sun-baked field to where the nearer of the remaining four squads was at work.

"Oh, put some pep into it, McPhee!" called the coach as he approached. "You all look as if you were asleep! Come on now! Wake up! Jones, get up there. You're away out of position. That's better. Now then, Quarter! Hold up! What's your down?"

"Third, sir, and four to go."

1

"All right. Show me what you're going to do with it. Head up, Martin! Look where you're going."

"36—27—43—86!" grunted the quarter-back. "36——"

"Signal!" cried Gordon, at right half.

McPhee straightened, cast a withering look at the half-back, wiped the perspiration from the end of his sun-burnt nose and repeated:

"36—27—43——"

Gordon shifted his feet, and—

"Hold up!" barked the coach. "Gordon, don't give the play away. Shifting your feet like that makes it a cinch for the other fellow. Get your position now and hold it until the ball's passed. All right. Once more, Quarter."

"36—27—43—86!" wailed McPhee. "36—27——"

The pigskin shot into his waiting hands, Gordon leaped forward, took it at a hand-pass and ran out behind his line, left half in advance, turned sharply in and set the ball down.

"First down!" called McPhee. "Sturges over."

"Hold up! Try a forward pass, McPhee. You're on the ten yards and it's third down. Get into this, you ends. Put some pep into it!"

"Signal! Martin back! 37—32—14—71—Hep!" The backs jumped to the left one stride. "37—32——"

Back flew the ball to the full-back, right end shot out and down the field across the mythical last line, the defence surged against the imaginary enemy and Martin, poising the ball at arm's length, threw over the line to Lee.

"All right," commented the coach. "That'll be all for today. Trot all the way in, fellows."

Five minutes later the field was empty of the sixty-odd boys who had reported for the second day's practice and the sun was going down behind the tree-clad hill to the west. In the gymnasium was the sound of rushing water, of many voices and of scraping benches. Mr. Robey wormed his way through the crowded locker-room to where Danny Moore, the trainer, stood in the doorway of the rubbing-room in talk with Jim Morton, this year's manager of the team. Morton was nineteen, tall, thin and benevolent looking behind a pair of rubber-rimmed spectacles.

"Did you put them on the scales, Dan?" asked the coach.

"Sure, the first, second and third, sir. Some of 'em dropped a good three pounds today. By gorry, I feel like I'd dropped that much meself!"

2

"It certainly is warm. Look here, Jim, is this all we get to work on? How many were out today?"

"Sixty-two, Coach. That's not bad. I suppose there'll be a few more dribble along tomorrow and the next day."

"Well, they look pretty fair, don't you think? Some of the new fellows seem to have ideas of football. All the last year fellows on hand?"

"All but Gilbert. He hasn't shown up. I don't know why, I'm sure."

"Better look him up," said the coach. "Gilbert ought to make a pretty good showing this year, and we aren't any too strong on guards."

"Gilbert rooms with Tim Otis, I think," replied Morton. "Oh, Tim! Tim Otis!"

A light-haired boy of seventeen, very straight, and very pink where an enormous bath-towel failed to cover him, wormed his way to them.

"Say, Tim, what's the matter with Gilbert?" asked Morton. "Isn't he coming out?"

Tim Otis shrugged a pair of broad, lean shoulders. "He hasn't got here yet, Morton. I don't know what's happened. He wrote me two weeks ago that he'd meet me at the station in New York yesterday for the three-fifty-eight, but he wasn't there and I haven't heard a word from him."

"Probably missed his connection," suggested Morton. "He lives out West somewhere, doesn't he?"

"Yes, Osawatomie, Kansas."

"It probably takes a good while to get away from a place with a name like that," said Mr. Robey drily. "Well, when he shows up, Otis, tell him to get a move on if he wants a place."

"Yes, sir, I will. I'm pretty certain he will be along today some time. I wouldn't be surprised if he was here now."

"All right. By the way, Otis, how do you feel at right half? Seem strange to you?"

"No, sir, I don't notice it. I did play right, you know, two years ago on the second. Seems to me it's easier to take the ball from that position, too."

"Well, don't try the fool trick your side-partner did today," said Mr. Robey, smiling. "Putting the ball under your elbow for a line plunge is a fine piece of business for a fellow who's been playing three years!"

Tim laughed. "I guess he did that because it was just practice, sir. He knows a lot better than to do it in scrimmage."

3

"I hope so. Well, hurry Gilbert along, will you? If he doesn't get out here inside of a few days he won't find much of a welcome, I'm afraid. I'm not going to keep positions open for anyone this year, not with the first game coming along in four days!"

"Don't you worry, Mr. Robey," replied Tim, with a chuckle and a flash of white teeth. "I'll have him out here the first day he shows up, even if I have to lug him all the way. Don't think I'll have to, though, for you couldn't keep Don from playing football unless you tied him up!"

"Nice chap," commented Morton, nodding at Tim as the latter returned to his bench. "Awfully clean-cut sort."

"A fine lad," agreed Danny Moore, and Mr. Robey nodded thoughtfully.

"I don't believe we're going to miss Kendall and Freer as much as I thought," he said after a moment. "Otis looks to me like a fellow who will stand a lot of work and grow on it. Well, I'm going to get a shower and get out of this sweat-box. As soon as you get time, Jim, I wish you'd catalogue the players the way we did last year and let me have the list. You know how Black did it, don't you?"

"Yes, sir. I'll have the list ready for you tomorrow."

"Good! Got a towel I can use, Dan? I haven't brought any yet. Thanks." The coach nodded and sought a place to disrobe. The trainer's gaze followed him until he was lost to sight beyond the throng.

"I wonder will he put it over again this year," he mused.

"Surest thing you know," asserted Morton. "Think I'm going to have the team licked the year I'm manager, Danny? Not so you'd notice it!"

"Well, between you and him," chuckled Danny, "I've no doubt you'll turn out a fine team. Say, he's the lad that can do it, though, now ain't he? Four years he's been at it, and it's fifty-fifty now, ain't it?"

"Yes, we lost the first two years and won last year and the year before. It was Andy Miller's team that started the ball rolling for us. No one could have won those first two years, anyhow, Danny. Robey had to start at the bottom and build up the whole thing. We hadn't been playing football here for several years before that. It takes a couple of years at the least to get a foundation laid. If we win this year we'll have something to boast of. No other team ever beat Claflin three times running."

"Maybe we won't either. I'm hoping we do, though. Still and all, it don't do to win too many times. You get to thinking you can't lose, d'ye see, and the first thing anyone knows you're all shot to pieces. I've seen it happen, me boy."

"Oh, I dare say, Danny, but don't let's start the losing streak until next year. I want to manage a winning team. Well, so long. See about some cooler weather tomorrow, will you?"

"I will so," replied the little trainer gravely. "I'll start arrangements to once."

Meanwhile Tim Otis, again arrayed in grey flannels and a pair of tan, rubber-soled shoes rather the worse for a hard summer, was on his way along the Row to the last of the five buildings set end to end on the brow of the hill. As he swung in between Wendell and Torrence—the gymnasium stood behind Wendell, and, save for the Cottage, as the principal's residence was called, was the only building out of alignment—he saw the entrances to dormitories and Main Hall thronged with youths who evidently preferred the coolness of outdoors to the heat of the rooms, while others were seated on the grass along the walk. It almost seemed that the entire roster of some one hundred and eighty students was before him. He answered many hails, but declined all inducements to tarry, keeping on his way past Main Hall and Hensey until Billings was reached. There he turned in and tramped to the right along the first floor corridor to the open door of Number 6, a room on the back of the building that looked out upon the tennis courts and, beyond, the football and baseball fields. From the fact that no sound came from the room, Tim decided that Don Gilbert had, after all, and in spite of what Tim called a "hunch," failed to arrive. But when he entered his mistake was instantly apparent. A maroon-coloured cushion hurtled toward him, narrowly missing the green shade of the droplight on the study table and, thanks to prompt and instinctive action on the part of Tim, sailed on, serene and unimpeded, into the corridor. Whereupon Tim uttered a savage whoop of mingled joy and vengeance and, traversing the length of the room in four leaps, hurled himself upon the occupant of the window-seat.

CHAPTER II
IN NUMBER SIX

FOR a long minute confusion and the noise of battle reigned supreme. Then, in response to a sudden yelp of pain from Don, Tim

5

drew off, panting and grinning. Don was extending a left hand, funereally wrapped in a black silk handkerchief, further along the window-seat and away from the scene of action.

"Hello!" said Tim. "What's the matter with that?"

"Hurt it a little," replied Don.

"Well, I supposed you had, you idiot! How? Hit it against your head?"

The other smiled in his slow fashion. "We had a sort of a wreck coming on. Out in Indiana somewhere. I got this. That's why I'm behind time."

"I'm beastly sorry, old man! I didn't notice the crêpe. Did I hurt it much!"

"No. I yelled so you wouldn't. Preparedness, you know. Safety first and so on. It isn't much. How's everything here?"

Tim seated himself at the other end of the seat, took his knees in his hands, and beamed.

"Oh, fine! Say, I'm tickled to death to see your ugly mug again, Don. You aren't a bit handsomer, are you?"

"I've been told I was. Trouble with you is, you don't recognise manly beauty when you see it."

"Oh, don't I?" Tim twirled an imaginary moustache. "I recognise it every time I look in the glass! Well, how are you aside from the bum fist?"

"Great! I've just had a séance with Josh. I tried to register and sneak by, but Brooke wouldn't have it that way. 'Er, quite so, Gilbert, quite so, but I—er—think you had better see Mr. Fernald.' So I did, and Josh read me the riot act. Thought for awhile he was going to send me home again."

"But didn't you tell him your train was wrecked?"

"Yes, but he didn't believe in it much. Thought I was romancing, I guess. Got a railway guide and showed me how I might have got here on time just the same. Maybe he's right, but I couldn't figure it out in Cincinnati. Besides, I didn't get away with much of anything besides pajamas and overcoat and shoes, and so I had to refit. That lost me the first connection and then I got held up again at Pittsburg. So here I am, the late Mr. Gilbert."

"Josh is an idiot," said Tim disgustedly. "Didn't he see your hand? How did he think you did that if you weren't in a wreck?"

"Oh, I kept that in my pocket and I guess he didn't notice it. He came around all right in the end, though. We parted friends. At least, I did."

"Well, what about that?" Tim nodded at the injured hand. "How'd you cut you, burn you?"

6

"Yes. Things got on fire."

"You're the most vivid descriptionist I ever listened to! Come across with the sickening details. How did it happen? I didn't see anything about it in the papers."

"Probably wasn't on the sporting page," replied Don gravely.

"Oh, dry up and blow away! Wasn't it in the papers?"

"Cincinnati papers had it. I haven't read the others. It wasn't much of a wreck really. Engineer killed, fireman scalded, about twenty passengers injured more or less. Several considerably more. Express messenger expected to pass out. Just a nice, cosy little wreck with no—no spectacular features, as you might say."

"Well, come on! How did it happen?"

"Freight train taking a siding and went to sleep at it. Our engine bumped the other engine and they both went smash. Hot coals and steam and so on got busy. It was about five in the morning. Just getting lightish. Everyone snuggled up in bed. Biff! Wow! I landed out on the floor on my hands and knees. Everyone yelled. Car turned half over and sat that way. Doors got jammed. We beat it out by the windows. I was a Roman Senator with a green berth curtain wrapped about me. Afterwards I sneaked back and pulled out my shoes and overcoat. Always sleep with my shoes under my pillow, you see. Good idea, too. If I hadn't had them there I'd never have got them. Couldn't get my bag out. Car was on fire by that time. Three others, too. They saved all but the one I was in and the express and baggage cars. After awhile a wrecking train came and then a lot of us walked to a village about a mile and a half away and had breakfast and went on to Cincinnati about noon."

"Gee! But, still, you know, I don't see how you got burned."

"Well, things were pretty hot. Some of them got burned a lot worse than I did. Had to pull some of them out the windows and through the roofs. Women, too. Lucky thing our car had only two in it. Two women, I mean. Things were fairly busy for awhile."

"Must have been. The engineer was killed straight off, eh?"

"Ours was. The other one managed to jump. Firemen got off all right, too. The other fireman. Ours got caught and scalded like the dickens. Saw the engineer myself." Don frowned and shuddered. "Nasty mess he was, too, poor fellow. Let's talk about something else. I don't like to remember that engineer."

"Too bad! But, say, you were lucky, weren't you? You might have been killed, I suppose."

"Might have, maybe. Didn't come very near it, though. First wreck I ever saw and don't want to see any more. Funny thing, though, I didn't mind it at all until I was on the train going to

Cincinnati. Excitement, I suppose. Then I came near keeling over, honest! What do you know about that, Timmy?"

"I guess anyone would have. How bad is your burn?"

"Not bad. Hurts a bit, though. It's the inside of the fingers and the palm. It'll be all right in a few days, I guess. Doctor chap said I'd have to have it dressed every day for awhile."

"But, Great Scott, Don, what about football?"

"I've thought of that. Nothing doing for a week or so, I guess. Rotten luck, eh?"

"Beastly! And Robey was telling me only half an hour ago to hurry you up. Said you'd have to come right out if you wanted a place. Still, when he understands what the trouble is——"

"I'll see him tonight, I guess. Who's playing guard, Tim?"

"Joe Gafferty, left; Tom Hall, right. Walton and Pryme and Lawton are all after places. Walton's been doing good work too, I think."

"All the fellows back?"

"Every last one. Remember Howard, who played sub half-back for the second last year? He's showing great form. Still, you can't tell much yet. There's to be scrimmage tomorrow. We play Thacher Saturday, you know. Sort of quick work and I don't believe we'll be anywhere near ready for them."

"Thacher's easy. We beat them 26 to 3 last year."

"Twenty-three to three."

"Twenty-six."

"Twenty-three. Bet you!"

"I don't bet, Timmy. Know I'm right, though. Anyway, Thacher's easy. Tell me the news."

"Oh, there isn't anything startling. We had the usual polite party at Josh's last night. Shook hands with the new chaps and told 'em how tickled we were to see them. Ate sandwiches and cake and lemonade and—by the way, we've got a new master; physics; Moller his name is; Caleb Moller, B.A. Quite a handsome brute and a swell dresser. Comes from Lehigh or one of those Southern colleges, I believe."

"Lehigh's in Pennsylvania, you ignoramus."

"Is it?" answered Tim untroubledly. "All right. Let it stay there. Anyhow, Caleb is some cheese."

"Where's Rollinson gone?"

"Don't know what happened to Rollo. Draper said he heard he'd gone to some whopping big prep school up in New Hampshire or somewhere."

"Or some other Southern school," suggested Don soberly.

8

"Dry up! And, say, get a move on. It's nearly time for eats and I'm starved."

"Timmy, I never saw the time you weren't starved. All right. I'm sort of hungry myself. Haven't had anything since about ten o'clock this morning. Ran out of money. Got here with eight cents in my pocket. That and my tuition check. I'd have cashed that if I could have and had a dinner. I was sure hungry!"

"Well, wash your dirty face and hands," said Tim, "and come along. Oh, say, Don, wait till you see the classy Norfolk suit I've got. I enticed dad into Crook's when we struck the city; told him I had to have some hankies and ties, you know. Then I steered him up against this here suit, and this here suit made a hit with him right away. If he could have got into it himself he'd have walked out in it. It's sort of green with a reddish thread wandering carelessly through it. It's some apparel, take it from me."

"Maybe I will if it fits me," responded Don.

"Will what?"

"Take it from you."

"Gee, but you're bright! Getting wrecked's put an edge on you, sonny. I'm afraid that suit wouldn't fit you, though, Don. You've grown about an inch since Spring, haven't you? You're beastly fat, too."

"I am not," denied Don, good-humouredly indignant. "I've kept in strict training all summer. What you think is fat is good hard muscle, Timmy. Feel of that arm if you don't believe it."

"Yes, quite village-blacksmithy."

"Quite what?"

"Village-blacksmithy. 'The muscles of his mighty arms were strong as iron bands,' or something like that. Get out of the way and let me wash up."

Don retired to his dresser and passed the brushes over his brown hair and snugged his tie up a bit. The face that looked back at him from the mirror was not, perhaps, handsome, although it by no means merited Tim's aspersions. There was a nice pair of dark brown eyes, rather slumberous looking, a nose a trifle too short for perfection and a mouth a shade too wide. But it was a good-tempered, pleasant face, on the whole, intelligent and capable and matching well the physically capable body below, a body of wide shoulders and well-knit muscles and a deep chest that might have belonged to a youth of eighteen instead of seventeen. Compared with Tim Otis, who was of the same age, Don Gilbert suffered on only two counts—quickness and vivacity. Tim, well-muscled, possessed a litheness that Don could never attain to, and moved,

9

thought and spoke far more quickly. In height Don topped his friend by almost a full inch and was broader and bigger-boned. They were both, in spite of dissimilarity, fine, manly fellows.

Tim, wiping his hands after ablutions, turned to survey Don with a quizzical smile on his good-looking face. And, after a moment's reflective regard of his chum's broad back, he broke the silence.

"Say, Don," he asked, "glad to get back?"

Don turned, while a slow smile crept over his countenance.

"Su-u-re," he drawled.

CHAPTER III
AMY HOLDS FORTH

BRIMFIELD ACADEMY is at Brimfield, and Brimfield is a scant thirty miles out of New York City and some two or three miles from the Sound. It is more than possible that these facts are already known to you; if you live in the vicinity of New York they certainly are. But at the risk of being tiresome I must explain a little about the school for the benefit of those readers who are unacquainted with it. Brimfield was this Fall entering on its twenty-fifth year, a fact destined to be appropriately celebrated later on. The enrollment was one hundred and eighty students and the faculty consisted of twenty members inclusive of the principal, Mr. Joshua L. Fernald, A.M., more familiarly known as "Josh." The course covers six years, and boys may enter the First Form at the age of twelve. Being an endowed institution and well supplied with money under the terms of the will of its founder, Brimfield boasts of its fine buildings. There are four dormitories, Wendell, Torrence, Hensey and Billings, all modern, and, between Torrence and Hensey, the original Academy Building now known as Main Hall and containing the class rooms, school offices, assembly room and library. The dining hall is in Wendell, the last building on the right. Behind Wendell is the gymnasium. Occupying almost if not quite as retiring a situation at the other end of the Row, is the Cottage, Mr. Fernald's residence. Each dormitory is ruled over by a master. In Billings Mr. Daley, the instructor in modern languages, was in charge at the period of this story, and since it was necessary to receive permission before leaving the school grounds after supper, Don and Tim paused at Mr.

Daley's study on the way out. Don's knock on the portal of Number 8 elicited an instant invitation to enter and a moment later he was shaking hands with the hall master, a youngish man with a pleasant countenance and a manner at once eager and embarrassed. Mr. Daley was usually referred to as Horace, which was his first name, and, as he shook hands, Don very nearly committed the awful mistake of calling him that! After greetings had been exchanged Don explained somewhat vaguely the reason for his tardy arrival and then requested permission to visit Coach Robey in the village after supper.

"Yes, Gilbert, but—er—be back by eight, please. I'm not sure that Mr. Robey isn't about school, however. Have you inquired?"

"No, sir, but Tim says he isn't eating in hall yet, and so——"

"Ah, in that case perhaps not. Well, be back for study hour. If you're going to supper I'll walk along with you, fellows." Mr. Daley closed his study door and they went out together and, as they trod the flags of the long walk that passed the fronts of the buildings, Mr. Daley discoursed on football with Tim while Don replied to the greetings of friends. They parted from the instructor at the dining hall door and sought their places at table, Don's arrival being greeted with acclaim by the other half-dozen occupants of the board. Once more he was obliged to give an account of himself, but this time his narrative was considered to be sadly lacking in detail and it was not until Tim had come to his assistance with a highly coloured if not exactly authentic history of the train-wreck that the audience was satisfied. Don told him he was an idiot. Tim, declining to argue the point, revenged himself by stealing a slice of Don's bread when the latter's attention was challenged by Harry Westcott at the farther end of the table.

Westcott, who was one of the editors of the school monthly, The Review, had developed the journalistic instinct to a high degree of late and had visions of a thrilling story in the November issue. But Don utterly refused to pose as a hero of any sort. The best Harry could get out of him was the acknowledgment that he had seen several persons removed from the wreck and had helped carry one to the relief train later. That wasn't much to go on, and, subsequently, Harry regretfully abandoned his plan.

After supper Don and Tim walked down to the village and Don had a few minutes of talk with the coach. Mr. Robey was sympathetic but annoyed. Although he didn't say so in so many words he gave Don to understand that he had failed in his duty to the school and the team in allowing himself to become concerned in a train-wreck. He didn't explain just how Don could have avoided it, and Don didn't think it worth while to inquire.

"You have that hand looked after properly and regularly, Gilbert," he said, "and watch practice until you can put on togs. Losing a week or so is going to handicap you. No doubt about that. And I'm not making any promises. But you keep your eyes open and maybe there'll be a place for you when you're ready to work. It's awfully hard luck, old chap. See you tomorrow."

Don went back to school through the warm dusk slightly cast down, although he had previously realised that football would be beyond him for at least a week. It is sometimes one thing to acknowledge a fact oneself and another to hear the same fact stated by a second person. There's a certain finality about the latter that is convincing. But if Don was downcast he didn't show it to his companion. Don had a way of concealing his emotions that Tim at once admired and resented. When Tim felt blue—which was mighty seldom—he let it be known to the whole world, and when he felt gay he was just as confiding. But Don—well, as Tim often said, he was "worse than an Indian!"

After study they sallied forth again, arm in arm, and went down the Row to Torrence and climbed the stairs to Number 14. As the door was half open knocking was a needless formality— especially as the noise within would have prevented its being heard—and so Tim pushed the portal further ajar and entered, followed by Don, on a most animated scene. Eight boys were sprawled or seated around the room, while another, a thin, tall, unkempt youth with a shock of very black hair which was always falling over his eyes and being brushed aside, was standing in a small clearing between table and windows balancing a baseball bat, surmounted by two books and a glass of water, on his chin. So interested was the audience in this startling feat that the presence of the new arrivals passed unnoted until the juggler, suddenly stepping back, allowed the law of gravity to have its way for an instant. Then his right hand caught the falling bat, the two books crashed unheeded to the floor and his left hand seized the descending tumbler. Simultaneously there was a disgruntled yelp from Jim Morton and a howl of laughter from the rest of the audience. For the juggler, while he had miraculously caught the tumbler in mid-air, had not been deft enough to keep the contents intact and about half of it had gone into the football manager's face. However, everyone there except Morton applauded enthusiastically and hilariously, and Larry Jones, sweeping his offending locks aside with the careless and impatient grace of a violin virtuoso, bowed repeatedly.

12

"Great stuff," approved Amory Byrd, rescuing his books from the floor. "Do it again and stand nearer Jim."

"If he does it again I'm going into the hall," said Morton disgustedly, wiping his damp countenance on the edge of Clint Thayer's bedspread. "You're a punk juggler, Larry."

"All right, you do it," was the reply. Larry proffered the bat and tumbler, but Morton waved them indignantly aside.

"I don't do monkey-tricks, thanks. Gee, my collar's sopping wet!"

"Oh, that's all right," called someone. "You'll be going to bed soon. Say, Larry, do that one with the three tennis balls."

"Isn't room enough. I know a good trick with coins, though. Any fellow got two halves?"

Groans of derision were heard and at that moment someone discovered the presence of Don and Tim and Larry's audience deserted him. When the new-comers had found accommodations, such as they were, conversation switched to the all-absorbing subject of football. Most of the fellows assembled were members of the first or second teams: Larry Jones was a substitute half; Clint Thayer was first-choice left tackle; Steve Edwards, sprawled on Clint's bed, was left end and this year's captain; the short, sturdy youth in the Morris chair was Thursby, the centre; Tom Hall, broad of shoulders, was right guard; Harry Walton, slimmer and rangier, with a rather saturnine countenance, was a substitute for that position. Jim Morton was, as we know, manager, and only Amory— or "Amy"—Byrd and Leroy Draper, the tow-headed, tip-nosed youth sharing the Morris chair with Thursby, were, in a manner of speaking, non-combatants.

But being a non-combatant didn't prevent Amy Byrd from airing his views and opinions on the subject of football, and that he was now doing. "Every year," he protested, "I have to hear the same line of talk from you chaps. It's wearying, woesomely wearying. Now, as a matter of fact, every one of you knows that we've got the average material and that we'll go ahead and turn out an average team and beat Claflin as per usual. The only chance for argument is what the score will be. You fellows like to grouse and pretend every fall that the team's shot full of holes and that the world is a dark, dreary, dismal place and that winning from Claflin is only a hectic dream. For the love of lemons, fellows, chuck the undertaker stuff and cheer up. Talk about something interesting, or, if you must talk your everlasting football, cut out the sobs!"

"Oh, dry up, Amy," said Tom Hall. "You oughtn't to be allowed to talk. Someone stuff a pillow in his mouth. No one has said we were shot full of holes, but you can't get around the fact that we've lost a lot of good players and——"

"Oh, gee, he's at it again!" wailed Amy. "Yes, Thomas darling, you've lost two fellows out of the line and two out of the backfield and there's nothing to live for and we'd better poison ourselves off before defeat and disgrace come upon us. All is lost save honour! Ah, woe is me!"

"Cut it out, Amy," begged Edwards. "You don't know anything about football, you idiot."

"Two in the line and two in the backfield is good," jeered Tim. "We've lost Blaisdell and Innes and Tyler——"

"Never was any good," interpolated Amy.

"And Roberts and Marvin——"

"Carmine's better!"

"And Kendall and Harris!" concluded Tim triumphantly.

"Never mind, Timmy, you've still got me!" replied Amy sweetly. "Gee, to hear you rave you'd think the whole team had graduated!"

"So it has, practically!"

"Ah, yes, and I heard the same dope this time last year. We'd lost Miller and Sawyer and Williams and—and Milton and a dozen or two more and there wasn't any hope for us! And all we did was to go ahead and dodder along and beat Claflin seven to nothing! Not so bad for a lifeless corpse, what?"

Steve Edwards laughed. "Well, maybe we do talk trouble a good deal about this time of year. It's natural, I guess. You lose fellows who played fine ball last year and you can't see just at first how anyone can fill their places. Someone always does, though. That's the bully part of it. I dare say we'll manage to dodder along, as Amy calls it, and rub it into old Claflin as we've been doing."

"First sensible word I've heard tonight," said Amy approvingly. "I wouldn't kick so much if I only had to hear this sort of stuff occasionally, but I'm rooming with the original crêpe-hanger! Clint sobs himself to sleep at night thinking how terribly the dear old team's shot to pieces. If I remark in my optimistic, gladsome way, 'Clint, list how sweetly the birdies sing, and observe, I prithee, the sunlight gilding yon mountain peak,' Clint turns his mournful countenance on me and chokes out something about a weak backfield! Say, I'm gladder every day of my life that I stayed sane and——"

"Stayed what?" exclaimed Jim Morton incredulously.

"And didn't become obsessed with football mania!"

14

"Where do you get the words, Amy?" sighed Clint Thayer admiringly.

"Amy's the original phonograph," commented Tim. "Only he's an improvement on anything Edison ever invented. You don't have to wind Amy up!"

"No, he's got a self-starting attachment," chuckled Draper.

"Returning to the—the original contention," continued Amy in superb disdain of the low jests, "I'll bet any one of you or the whole kit and caboodle of you that we beat Claflin again this year. Now make a noise like some money!"

"Amy, we don't bet," remarked Tom Hall. "At least, not with money. Betting money is very wrong. (Amy sniffed sarcastically.) But I'll wager a good feed for the crowd that we have a harder time beating Claflin this year than we had last. And I'll——"

"Oh, piffle! I don't care whether you have to work harder to do it or not. I say you'll do it! Hard work wouldn't hurt you, anyway. You're a lot of loafers. All any of you do is go out to the field and strike an attitude like a hero. Why——"

Cries of expostulation and threats of physical violence failed to disturb the irrepressible Amy.

"Tell you what I'll do, you piffling Greeks, I'll blow you all off to a top-hole dinner at the Inn if Claflin beats us. There's a sporting proposition for you, you undertakers' assistants!"

"Yah! What do we do if she doesn't?" exclaimed Walton.

Amy surveyed him coldly. He didn't like Harry Walton and never attempted to disguise the fact. "Why, Harry, old dear, you'll just keep right on squandering your money as usual, I suppose. But I don't want you to waste any on me. This is a one-man wager."

"No, it isn't," said Leroy Draper, "I'm in on it, Amy. I'll take half of it."

"All right, Roy. But our money's safe as safe! This bunch of grousers won't get fat off us, old chap!"

"Say," said Walton, who had been trying to get Amy's attention for a minute, "what's the story about my squandering my money? Anybody seen you being careless with yours, Amy?"

"Not that I know of. I'm not careless with it; I'm careful. But being careful with money is different from having it glued to your skin so you have to have a surgical operation before——"

"Oh, cut it, Amy," said Tim.

"I spend my money just as freely as you do," returned Walton hotly. "You talk so much with your face——"

"Let it go at that, Harry," advised Tom Hall soothingly. "Amy's just talking."

"That's all," agreed Amy sweetly. "Just talking. You're the original little spendthrift, Harry. I'm going to write home to your folks some time and warn 'em. Hold on, you chaps, don't hurry off. The night is still in its infancy. Wait and watch it grow up. Steve! Sit down!"

"Thanks, I've got to be moseying along," replied Captain Edwards. "It's pretty near ten. I think it would be a rather good idea if we had a rule that football men were to be in their rooms at a quarter to ten all during the season."

"I can see that you're going to be one of these here martinets you read about," said Tim with a sigh. "Steve, remember you were young once yourself."

"He never was!" declared Amy with decision. "Steve was grown-up when he was quite young and he's never got over it. Thank the Fates I don't have to be bossed by him! Are you all leaving? Clint, count the spoons and forks! Come again, everyone. I've got lots more to say. Good-night, Don. Glad to see you back again, old sober-sides. Sorry about that fin of yours. Be careful with him, Tim. You know how it is with the dear old team. We need every man we can get. Hold on, Harry! Did you drop that quarter? Oh, I beg pardon, it's only a button. That's right, Thurs, kick the chair over if it's in your way. We don't care a bit about our furniture. For the love of lemons, Larry, don't grin like that! Think of the team, man! Remember your sorrows! Good-night!"

Half-way to Billings Don broke the silence.

"Fellows are funny, aren't they?" he murmured.

"Funny? How do you mean?" asked Tim.

"Oh, I don't know," replied Don after a thoughtful moment. "They're—they're so different, I guess."

"Who's different from who?"

"Everyone," answered Don, smothering a yawn.

Tim viewed him in the radiance of the light over the doorway with profound admiration. "Don, you're a brilliant chap! Honest, sometimes I wonder how you do it! Doesn't it hurt?"

Don only smiled.

CHAPTER IV
THE FIRST GAME

DON sat on the bench and watched the game with Thacher School. With him were nearly a dozen other substitutes, but they, unlike Don, were in football togs and might, in fact probably would, get into the game sooner or later. There was no such luck for Don so long as his hand remained swathed in bandages, and he was silently bewailing his luck. At his right sat Danny Moore, chin in hand and elbow in palm, viewing the contest from half-closed eyes. The trainer was small and red of hair and very freckled, and he was thoroughly Irish and, in the manner of his race, mightily proud of it. Also, he was a clever little man and a good trainer.

An attempted forward pass by the visitors grounded and the horn squawked the end of the first period. Danny turned his beady green eyes on Don. "Likely you're wishin' yourself out there with the rest of 'em, boy," he said questioningly.

Don nodded, smiled his slow smile and shook his head. "I guess I won't get into it for a week yet. Doc says this hand has got to do a lot of healing first. He has a fine time every day pulling and cutting the old skin off it. Guess he enjoys it so much he will hate to have it heal. I should think, Danny, that if I had a heavy glove, sort of padded in the palm, I might play a little."

"Sure, I'll fix you up something real nate," replied Danny readily. "Nate an' scientific, d'ye see? An' so soon as the Doc says the word you come to me an' I'll be having it ready for you."

"Will you? Thanks, Danny. That's great! I would like to get back to practice again. I'm afraid I'll be as stiff and stale as anything if I stay out much longer."

"Go easy on your eating, lad, and it'll take you no time at all to catch up with the rest of 'em. Spread this hand for me while I see the shape of it. What happened to your finger there?"

"I broke it when I was a little kid, playing baseball."

"Sure, whoever set it for you must have been cross-eyed," said the trainer, drily. "'Tis a bum job he did."

"Yes, it's a little crooked, but it works all right."

"You'd have hard work gettin' your engagement ring over that lump, I'm thinking. It's a fortunate thing you're not a girl, d'ye mind."

Don laughed. "Engagement rings go on the other hand, don't they, Danny?"

17

"Faith, I don't know. Bad luck to him, he's done it again!"

"Who? What?" asked Don startledly.

"Jim Morton. That's twice today he's spilled most of the water from the pail. Well, I'll have to go an' fill it, I suppose."

Danny went off to get the water bucket and the teams lined up again near the visitors' twenty-five yard line. Coach Robey had put in a somewhat patched-up team today. Captain Edwards was at left end, Clint Thayer at left tackle, Gafferty at left guard, Peters at centre, Pryme at right guard, Crewe at right tackle, Lee at right end, Carmine at quarter, St. Clair and Gordon at half and Martin at full. It was not the best line-up possible, but it was so far handling the situation fairly satisfactorily. The practice of the last two days had developed one or two strains and proved more than one of the first-choice fellows far below condition. Tim Otis was out for a day or two with a twisted knee and Tom Hall with a lame shoulder. Thursby had developed an erratic streak the day before and was nursing his chagrin further along the bench. Holt, the best right end, was in trouble with the faculty, and Rollins, full-back, had pulled a tendon in his ankle. A full team of second- and third-string players were having signal work on the practice gridiron.

In the stands a fairly good-sized gathering of onlookers was applauding listlessly at such infrequent times as the maroon-and-grey team gave it any excuse. Thus far, however, exciting episodes had been scarce. The weather, which was enervatingly warm, affected both elevens and the playing was sluggish and far from brilliant. The Brimfield backs, with the exception of Carmine, who was always on edge, conducted themselves as if they were at a rehearsal, accepting the ball in an indifferent manner and half-heartedly plunging at the opposing line or jogging around the ends. As the first half drew to a close both goal lines were still unthreatened and from all indications would remain so for the rest of the contest. A slight thrill was developed, though, just before the second period came to an end when a Thacher half-back managed to get away outside Crewe and romped half the length of the field before he was laid low by Carmine. After that there was an exchange of punts and the teams trotted off to the gymnasium.

Don left the bench with the others, but did not follow them to the dressing room. Instead, he strolled down the running track and across to the practice field, where Tim was superintending the signal practice. Don joined him and followed the panting, perspiring players down the field. Tim's conversation was rather difficult to follow, since he continually interrupted himself to instruct or admonish the toilers.

"I feel like a slave-driver, pushing these poor chaps around in this heat. How's the game going? No score? We must be playing pretty punk, I guess. What sort of a team has—Jones, you missed your starting signal again. For the love of mud, keep your ears open!—Thacher must be as bad as we are. Who's playing in my place? Gordon? Is he doing anything?—Try them on that again, McPhee, will you? Robbins, you're supposed to block hard on that and not let your man through until the runner's got into the line.—I could have played today all right, but that idiot, Danny, wouldn't let me. My knee's perfectly all right."

"Then why do you limp?" asked Don innocently.

"Force of habit," said Tim. "What time is it?"

Don consulted his silver watch and announced a quarter to four.

"Thank goodness! That'll do, fellows. You'd better get your showers before you try to see that game. If Danny catches you over there the way you are he will just about scalp you! By the way, McPhee, you saw what I meant about that end-around play, didn't you? You can't afford to slow up the play by waiting for your end to get to you. He's got to be in position to take the pass at the right second. Otherwise they'll come through on you and stop him behind the line. There ought to be absolutely no pause between Smith's pass to you and your pass to Compton, or whoever the end is. You get the ball, turn quick, toss it to the end and fall in behind him. It ought to be almost one motion. Of course, I know you fellows were pretty well fagged today, but you don't want to let your ends think they can take their time on that play, old man, for it's got to be fast or it's no earthly good. Thus endeth the lesson. Come on, Don, and we'll go over and add the dignity of our presence to that little affair."

They reached the bench just as the two teams trotted back and Brimfield's supporters raised a faint cheer. Don imagined that there was a little more vim in the way the maroon-and-grey warriors went into the field for the second half and the results proved him right.

It was the home team's kick-off, and after Captain Edwards, in the absence of Hall, had sped the ball down to Thacher's twenty yards and a Thacher player had sped it back to the thirty, Brimfield settled down to business. Probably Coach Robey's remarks in the interim had been sufficiently caustic to get under the skin. At all events Brimfield forced Thacher to punt on third down and then almost blocked the kick. As it was, the ball hurtled out of bounds near the middle of the field and became Brimfield's on her forty-eight. Two plunges netted five yards, and then St. Clair, returning to form, ripped his way past tackle on the left and fought over two

19

white lines before he was halted. Gordon and Martin made it first down in three tries and Carmine worked the left end for four more. Thacher stiffened then, however, and after two ineffectual plunges St. Clair punted and Brimfield caught on her goal line and ran back a dozen yards, Lee, right end, missing his tackle badly and Steve Edwards being neatly blocked off. But Thacher found the going even harder than her opponent had and in a moment she, too, was forced to punt.

This time it was St. Clair who caught and who, eluding both Thacher ends, ran straight along the side line until he was upset near the enemy's thirty-five yards. As he went down he managed to get one foot over the line and the referee paced in fifteen yards, set the ball to earth and waved toward the Thacher goal.

Martin faked a forward pass and the ball went to Gordon for a try at right tackle. Thayer and Gafferty opened a fine hole there and Gordon romped through and made eight before the Thacher secondary defence brought him down. Martin completed the distance through centre. From the twenty-four yards to the ten the ball went, progress, however, becoming slower as the attack neared the goal. On a shift that brought Thayer to the right side of the line, St. Clair got around the short end for three and Martin added two more, leaving the pigskin on the five-yard line. It was third down and Martin went back to kick. But after a moment's hesitation Carmine changed his signals and the ends stole out toward the side lines. Thacher proceeded to arrange her forces to intercept a forward pass and again Carmine switched. The ends crept back and Martin retired to the fifteen-yard line and patted the turf. Carmine knelt in front of him and eyed the goal. Then the signals came again, and with them the ball, and it was Martin who caught it and not Carmine. Two steps to the right, a quick heave, a frenzied shouting from the defenders of the goal, a confused jostling, and Captain Edwards, one foot over the line, reached his arms into the air, pulled down the hurtling pigskin, tore away from one of the enemy, lunged forward and went down under a mass of bodies, but well over the goal line.

Brimfield found her enthusiasm then, and her voice, and cheered loudly and long, only ceasing when Carmine walked out with the ball under his arm and flung himself to the turf opposite the right hand goal post. Thursby, hustled in by Coach Robey, measured distance and direction, stepped forward and, as the line of Thacher warriors swept forward with upstretched hands, swung his toe against the ball and sent it neatly across the bar.

With the score seven to nothing against her, Thacher returned

20

to the fray with a fine determination, but, when the teams had changed places after the kick-off and the last period had begun, she speedily found that victory was not to be her portion. Mr. Robey sent in nearly a new team during that last ten minutes and the substitutes, fresh and eager, went at it hammer-and-tongs. Thacher enlisted fresh material, too, but it couldn't stop the onslaught that soon took the ball down the field to within close scoring distance of her goal. That Brimfield did not add another touchdown was only because her line, overanxious, was twice found off-side and penalised. Even then the ball went at last to within six inches of the goal line and it was only after the nimble referee had dug into the pile-up like a terrier scratching for a bone in an ash-heap that the fact was determined that Thacher had saved her bacon by the width of the ball. She kicked out of danger from behind her goal and after two plays the final whistle blew.

It was a very hot and very weary crowd of fellows who thronged the dressing room in the gymnasium five minutes later and, above the swish of water in the showers, shouted back and forth and discussed the game from as many angles as there had been participants. Possibly Brimfield had no very good reason for feeling proud of her afternoon's work, for last year she had defeated Thacher 26 to 3. That game, however, had taken place two weeks later in the season, when the Maroon-and-Grey was better off in the matter of experience, and so perhaps was not a fair comparison. At all events, Brimfield liked the way she had "come back" in that third period and liked the way in which the substitutes had behaved, and displayed a very evident inclination to pat herself on the back.

Tim, who had haled Don into the gymnasium on the way back to hall, tried his best to convince all those who would listen to him that they had played a perfectly punk game and that nothing but the veriest fluke had accounted for that score. But they called him a "sore-head" and laughed at him, and even drove him away with flicking towels, and he finally gave it up and consented to accompany Don back to Billings, limping a trifle whenever he thought no one was looking.

Don missed Tim at supper, for the training tables started that evening and Tim went off to one of them with his napkin ring and his own particular bottle of tomato catsup, leaving his chum feeling forlornly "out of it."

CHAPTER V
DON GOES TO THE SECOND

LIFE at Brimfield Academy settled down for Don into the accustomed routine. The loss of one day made no difference in the matter of lessons, for with Tim's assistance—they were both in the Fifth Form—he easily made up what had been missed. They were taking up German that year for the first time and Don found it hard going, but he managed to satisfy Mr. Daley after a fashion. Don was a fellow who studied hard because he had to. Tim could skim his lessons, make a good showing in class and remember enough of what he had gone over to appear quite erudite. Don had to get right down and grapple with things. He once said enviously, and with as near an approach to an epigram as he was capable of, that whereas Tim got his lessons by inhaling them, he, Don, had to chew them up and swallow them! But when examination time came Don's method of assimilation showed better results.

The injured hand healed with incredible slowness, but heal it did, and at last the day came when the doctor consented to let his impatient pupil put on the padded arrangement that the ingenious Danny Moore had fashioned of a discarded fielder's glove and some curled hair, and Don triumphantly reported for practice. His triumph was, however, short-lived, for Coach Robey viewed him dubiously and relegated him to the second squad, from which Mr. Boutelle was then forming his second team. "Boots" was a graduate who turned up every Fall and took charge of the second or scrub team. It was an open secret that he received no remuneration. Patriotism and sheer love of the game were the inducements that caused Mr. Boutelle to donate some two months of time and labour to the cause of turning out a second team strong enough to give the first the practice it needed. And he always succeeded. "Boutelle's Babies," as someone had facetiously termed them, could invariably be depended on to give the school eleven as hard a tussle as it wanted—and sometimes a deal harder. Boots was a bit of a driver and believed in strenuous work, but his charges liked him immensely and performed miracles of labour at his command. His greeting of Don was almost as dubious as had been Coach Robey's.

"Of course I'm glad to have you, Gilbert, but the trouble is that as soon as we've got you nicely working Mr. Robey will take you away. That's a great trick of his. He seems to think the purpose of the second team is to train players for the first. It isn't, though. He gives me what he doesn't want every year and I do my best to make a team from it, and I ought to be allowed to keep what I make. Well, never mind. You do the best you can while you're with us, Gilbert."

"Maybe he won't have me this year," said Don dejectedly. "He seems to think that being out for a couple of weeks has queered me."

"Well, you don't feel that way about it, do you?"

"No, sir, I'm perfectly all right. I've watched practice every afternoon and I've been doing a quarter to a half on the track."

"Hm. Well, you've got a little flesh that will have to come off, but it won't take long to lose it this weather. Sit down a minute." They were in front of the stand and Mr. Boutelle seated himself on the lower tier and Don followed his example. "Let me see, Gilbert. Last year you played left guard, didn't you?"

"Yes, sir."

"And if I remember aright your chief difficulty was in the matter of weight."

"I'm twelve pounds heavier this fall, sir."

"Yes, but some of that'll come off, I guess. However, that doesn't matter. You were getting along pretty well at the last of the season, I remember. Who's ahead of you on the first?"

"Well, Gafferty's got the first choice, I guess. And then there's Harry Walton."

"You can beat Walton," said Boots decisively. "Walton lacks head. He can't think things out for himself. You can. What you'll have to do this year, my boy, is speed up a little. It took you until about the middle of the season to find your pace. Remember?"

"Yes, sir, I know."

"Well, you won't stay with us long, as I've said, and so I'm not going to build you into the line, Gilbert. I've got some good-looking guard material and I can't afford to work over you and get dependent on you and then have Robey snatch you away about the middle of the fall. That won't do. But I'll tell you what we will do, Gilbert. We'll use you enough to bring you around in form slowly. You'll play left guard for awhile every day. But what I want you to really do is to help with the others. You've been at it two years now and you know how the position ought to be played and you've got hard common-sense. I'll put the guard candidates in your hands. See what you can do with them. There's a couple of likely chaps in Kirkwell and Merton, and there are two or three more after positions. You take them in charge, Gilbert, and show me what you know about coaching. What do you say?"

"Why, Mr. Boutelle, I—I don't know that I can show anyone

else what to do. I can play the position myself after a fashion, but—well, I guess it's another thing to teach, isn't it?"

"Oh, I don't know. It is if you go into it with the idea that it is, but don't do that. Play the position as it ought to be played, tell the others why, call them down when they make mistakes, pat them on the back when they do right. Just forget that you're trying to teach. If a fellow came to you and said: 'Gilbert, I want to play guard but I don't know how, and I wish you'd tell me how you do it,' why, you wouldn't have any trouble, would you?"

"N-no, sir, I guess not," replied Don a trifle doubtfully.

"Well, there you are. Try it, anyway. You'll get on all right. I'll be right on hand to dig the spurs in when your courage fails." Mr. Boutelle smiled. "We're going to have a dandy second team this fall, my boy. We've got nothing to build on, only a lot of green material, and that's the best part of it. I don't care how inexperienced the material is if it's willing to learn and has the usual number of arms and legs and such things and a few ounces of grey matter in the cranium. Well, here we go. Nothing today but passing and punting, I guess. Sure your hand's all right?"

"Yes, sir, thanks. I don't really need this contrivance; it's awfully clumsy; but Doc said I'd better wear it for a few days."

"Best to be on the safe side. I'll have you take one squad of these chaps, I guess, and I'll give the other to Lewis. You know the usual stuff, Gilbert. Rest 'em up now and then; they're soft and the weather's warm. But work 'em when they're working. Any fellow who soldiers gets bounced. All out, second squad!"

There wasn't anything that afternoon but the sort of drudgery that tries the enthusiasm of the tyro: passing the ball in circles, falling on it, catching it on the bound and starting. Don was surprised to discover how soft he was in spite of his daily exercise on the cinders. When the hour's practice was over he was just about as thankful as any of the puffing, perspiring youths around him. Considering it afterward, Don was unable to view the material with the enthusiasm Mr. Boutelle had displayed. To him the thirty-odd boys who had reported for the second team were a hopeless lot, barring, of course, a few, not more than four in all, who had had experience last season. In another week Mr. Robey would make a cut in the first squad and the second would find itself augmented by some ten or twelve cast-offs. But just now the second squad looked to Don to be a most unlikely lot. When he confided all this to Tim that evening the latter said:

"Don't you worry, old man. Boots will make a team out of them. Why, he could make a football team out of eleven clothing store dummies! Sometimes I think that Boots ought to be head coach instead of Robey. I've got nothing against Robey, either. He's a bit of a 'miracle man' himself, but for building a team out of nothing Boutelle has him both shoulders to the mat!"

"I don't believe Boots would want to coach the first," replied Don.

"Why not?"

"I don't know. He's sort of—well, he kind of likes to—Oh, I don't know."

"Very clearly explained, Donald."

"Well, Boots, if he was a soldier, would be the sort that would want to lead a charge where the odds were against him. See what I mean?"

"You mean he has a hankering for the forlorn chance business? Maybe so. That's not a bad name for the second, is it? The Forlorn Chances! I guess you've got him dead to rights, though. Boots is for the under dog every time. I guess coaching the first and having his pick of the players wouldn't make any sort of a hit with Boots. It would be too tame. Boots likes to take three discarded veterans, two crips and a handful of green youngsters and whittle them into a bunch that will make us sweat and toil to score on. And, what's more, he does it! Bet you anything, Don, this year's second will be every bit as good as last year's."

"I won't take it, because I think so myself," laughed Don. "I can't see how he's going to do it, Tim, but something tells me he will!"

"Oh, with you to coach the guards it will be no trick at all," said Tim, grinning.

Don smiled thinly. "I'll make an awful mess of it, I guess," he muttered.

"Not you, boy!" and Tim slapped him encouragingly on the back. "You'll blunder right ahead to glory, same as you always do. You'll make hard work of it and all that, but you'll get there. Don, you're exactly like the porpoise—no, the tortoise in the fable. You don't look fast, old man, but you keep on moving ahead and saying nothing and when the hares arrive you're curled up on the finish line fast asleep. Tortoises can't curl up, though, can they? And, say, what the dickens is a tortoise, anyway? I always get tortoises and porpoises mixed."

"A porpoise is a fish," replied Don gravely. "And a tortoise is a land turtle. But they're both anthropoids."

"Are they?" asked Tim vaguely. "All right. Here, what are you grinning at? Anthropoids nothing! An anthropoid is a monkey or—or something."

"You're an anthropoid yourself, Timmy."

"Meaning I'm a monkey?"

"Not at all. Here, look it up." And Don shoved a dictionary across the table. Tim accepted it suspiciously.

"All right," he said, "but if it's what I think it is you'll have to fight. Anthesis, anthropocosmic——Say, I'm glad you didn't call me that! Here it is. Now let's see. 'Anthropoid, somewhat like a human being in form or other characteristics'! Something like—— You wait till I get you in the tank again! 'Something like a human being'! For two cents I'd lay you on the bed and spank you with that tennis racket!"

"I've got two cents that say you can't do it," replied Don.

"Well, I could if there wasn't so much of you," grumbled Tim. "Now shut up and let me stuff awhile. Horace has been eyeing me in a way I don't like lately. How's your German going?"

"Not very well. It's a silly language, I think. But I guess I'll get the hang of it after awhile. What I want to know is why they can't make their letters the way we do."

"Because they're afraid someone might be able to read the plaguy stuff. Tell you what we'll do, Don."

"What'll we do?"

"We'll go for a swim in the tank after study. Will you?"

Don winked slowly. "Not after that threat, thanks."

"I won't touch you, honest to goodness, Don! Did you learn to swim any better this Summer?"

"Where would I learn?" asked the other. "There's no place to swim out my way, unless it's the river."

"Well, don't the rivers in Kansas contain water?"

"Yes, sometimes! Winter, usually. If you'll promise not to grab me when I'm not looking I'll go. I hate the taste of that tank water, Tim."

"You ought to know how to swim, old man. Never mind, Mr. Conklin will get hold of you this Winter and beat it into you."

"I can swim now," replied Don indignantly.

"Oh, yes, you can swim like a hunk of lead! The last time I saw you try it you did five strokes and then got so elated that you nearly drowned yourself trying to cheer! I could teach you in three lessons if you'd let me."

"Much obliged, but nothing doing, Timmy. I'd as lief drown by myself as have you hold my head under water."

"That was just a joke, Don. I won't ever do it again. I wanted you to get used to the water, you see."

"I don't mind getting used to it outside, but I hate to fill up with it, Tim. It tastes very nasty. You may be a good teacher, but I don't like your methods."

"Well, we'll go and have a dip, anyway," laughed Tim. "It'll set us up and refresh us after our arduous stuffing."

"If you don't cut out the chatter there won't be any stuffing," warned Don. "It's almost half-past now. And I've got three solid pages of this rot to do. Dry up, like a good pal."

CHAPTER VI
THE SEARCH OF ADVENTURE

BY that time Brimfield had played her second game and lost it, 6 to 14, to Canterbury High School. Canterbury was not considered very formidable and Brimfield usually had little trouble with her. But this year things had gone wrong from the start of the game to the finish, wrong, that is, from Brimfield's point of view. Fumbling had been much in evidence and poor judgment even more. Carmine had worked like a Trojan at quarter-back for two periods, but had somehow failed to display his usually good generalship, and McPhee, who had taken his place at the beginning of the second half, while he ran the team well, twice dropped punts in the backfield, one of which accounted for Canterbury's second touchdown and goal. Oddly enough, it was the veterans who failed most signally to live up to expectations, and of all the veterans Tom Hall was the worst offender. Possibly Tom's shoulder still bothered him, but even that couldn't have accounted for all his shortcomings. Crewe, who played tackle beside Tom, was not a very steady man, and Tom's errors threw him off his game badly, with the result that, until Coach Robey put Pryme in for Tom in the third period, Canterbury made a lamentable number of gains at the right of the Brimfield line. Even Tim Otis, usually undisturbed by anything short of an earthquake, was affected by the playing of the others and finally had what he called a "brain-storm" in the third period, getting the signals twisted and being thrown back for an eight-yard loss. That misadventure bothered him so that he was heartily glad when Gordon was rushed in a few minutes later.

The team took the beating to heart and the school at large was disposed to indulge in sarcasm and bitterness. Only Coach Robey seemed undisturbed. He lavished no praise, you may be sure, but, on the other hand, neither did he utter any criticism after the contest was over. Instead, he laid off more than half the line-up on Monday and Tuesday, and, since the weather continued almost unseasonably warm, the rest was just what the fellows needed. Wednesday's practice went with a new snap and vim and those who broiled in the afternoon sun and watched it found grounds for hope.

It was on Wednesday that Don began his connection with the second team, and by then the injured hand was so well along that he was able to discard the glove. Three days of kindergarten work followed, with, on Saturday, a short signal drill. The first team journeyed away that afternoon to play Miter Hill School, and Don would have liked very much to have gone along. But Boots put his charges through a good, hard hour and a half of work, and Don had all he could attend to at home. Just before supper he did, however, walk down to the station and meet Tim when the team arrived home. Tim, who seemed remarkably fresh for a youth who had played through the most of four ten-minute periods, scorned the coach and he and Don footed it back.

"Twenty to nothing, my boy," said Tim exultantly. "They never had a look-in. It was some game, believe me, dearie! And I want to tell you, too, that Miter Hill is fifty per cent better than Canterbury ever thought of being!"

"That's fine," said Don. "What sort of a game did you play?"

"Me? Oh, I was the life of the party. Got off two nice little runs, one for thirty and the other for forty-five yards. Got a touchdown the second time. I wouldn't have, though, if Steve hadn't paced me most the way down and put the quarter out. Old Steve played like a whirlwind today. We all did, I guess. There was only one fumble, and that wasn't anyone's fault. Holt got a forward pass and a Miter Hill chap plunged into him and just about knocked the breath out of him and he let go of the ball."

"Twenty to nothing? Three touchdowns, then."

"Yep, and Rollins only missed one goal. Rollins scored once, I scored once and Steve took over the last one."

"Forward pass?"

"No, end-around. It went off great, too. We were way back on the eighteen yards, I think it was, and we worked the fake forward pass play, with Steve taking the ball from Carmine. We fooled them finely. They never got onto it at all until Steve was over the line. Some of the fellows who were doing so much grousing last week

28

ought to have come along today and seen some real football. Robey was as pleased as anything. You could tell that because he looked sort of cross and told us how bad we were!"

"Wish I'd seen it," mourned Don.

"It was some game, all right, all right! We're going to have a modest celebration this evening; just Tom Hall and Clint Thayer and Hap Crewe, maybe, and yours truly. Better come along. Will you?"

"Where are you going?"

"Oh, just down to the village. We'll leave the window open."

"You'll get nabbed if you try that," demurred Don. "Better not, Tim."

"Well, we may be back by ten. No harm in having a way open in case something delays us, though. We'll have a little feed at the Inn, you know, and——"

"Don't be a chump," growled Don. "You're in training and you know mighty well Robey won't stand for any funny-business."

"What Robey doesn't know isn't going to hurt him," replied Tim untroubledly. "And he won't know anything about this because he's off for home on the seven o'clock train. Tom heard him tell Steve he wouldn't be back until Monday noon."

"Yes, but someone will see you and Robey'll hear of it. And then you'll get the dickens from him and be hauled up to the office. Better not risk it, Timmy."

"Gee, you're worse than Mr. Poe's crow! Or was it a raven? What's the difference, anyhow? Now don't tell me they're both anthropeds or pods, or whatever it is, because I'm onto you as a disseminator of knowledge! I never got even with you yet for calling me 'something like a human being'."

"I'll take it back, then; you aren't. But, just the same, Tim, I wish you'd cut out the celebration."

"You're all the time interfering with my innocent pleasures," protested Tim. "Why, bless you, dearie, we aren't going to cut-up. We're merely going to stroll quietly to the village, trolling a song, mayhap, and look in the windows."

"That'll take you a long time," Don laughed. "There are only half a dozen."

"Wrong. A fellow opened a watchmaker's emporium next door to the post office t'other day and has a most fascinating window. It has four alarm clocks, three pairs of cuff-links and a chronometer in it! Oh, it's swell! Do you realise, Don, that slowly but surely our little village is taking on the—the semblance of a metropolis? All we want is a movie palace!"

"Let's start one. They say there's a lot of money in them."

"Bet there is! We've got three or four at home, and they're peaches. Full every minute, too. I went a lot last Summer; had filmitis, I guess. But how about the party? Will you come along?"

"No, thanks."

"Oh, come on, Don! Have a heart! Be one of our merry gang."

"I'd rather not, thank you. I like Josh well enough, but I don't like to stand on the carpet and hear him say 'Until further notice, Gilbert.' Nothing doing, Tim!"

And Don remained adamant the rest of the way to school and while they made a hurried toilet and rushed to dining hall in an effort to reach it before the food gave out.

The team members received an ovation that evening when they entered the dining hall. It seemed as if the school wanted to make up for its unkindness of a week before. Some few of the fellows, recalling sarcastic comments overheard, were inclined to be haughty and unforgiving, but eventually they melted. Don, now at the second training-table, presided over by Mr. Boutelle, saw that Coach Robey's chair was vacant, which fact bore out Tim's statement that the coach had gone home over Sunday. But, even granting that, Don didn't approve of Tim's celebration, for, as he very well knew, after a football victory fellows were very likely to be carried away by their enthusiasm and to forget such trifling things as rules and regulations. He determined to try again to dissuade Tim after supper.

But Tim, who was in a very cheerful and expansive mood, refused to be dissuaded. Instead, he turned the tables and begged so hard for Don to come with him that Don finally relented. After all, there was no harm in the excursion if they got permission and were back in hall by ten o'clock. And it was a wonderfully pleasant, warm evening, much too fine an evening to spend indoors, and—well, secretly, Don wanted some fun as much as any of them, perhaps!

Permission was easily obtained and at seven they met Tom Hall and Clint Thayer in front of Torrence. Crewe failed them, but Tim said it didn't matter; that there were only four "Three Musketeers" anyhow! So they set off for the village in high spirits, through a warm, fragrant, star-lighted evening, with no settled plan of action in mind save to do about as they liked for the succeeding three hours. Clint Thayer had a strip of plaster across the saddle of his nose, which gave him a strangely benign expression. Tom walked a bit stiffly and confessed to "a peach of a shin," which probably meant something quite different from what it suggested. Only Tim, of the three first team fellows, had emerged unscathed, and he referred to the fact in an unpleasantly superior manner which brought from Tom Hall the remark that it was easy enough to get through a game without any knocks if you didn't do anything! Whereupon Tim flicked him across the cheek with an imaginary glove, the challenge was issued and accepted and the two fought an exciting duel with rapiers—as imaginary as the glove—on the sidewalk, feinting, thrusting, parrying, until Clint cried "The guard! The guard!" and they all raced down the road to the nearest lamp-post, where Tim insisted on looking to his wounds. To hear him tell it, he was as full of holes as a sieve, while, on the same authority, Tom was a dead man. Tom denied being dead, but Tim insisted and refused to pay any heed to him all the rest of the way to the village on the ground that, being dead, Tom had no business to talk.

But when they reached what Tim called "the heart of the city" Tom was allowed to come to life again. The heart of the city consisted of the junction of two village streets whereon were located the diminutive town hall, the post office, a fire house and five stores. They began with the druggist's, ranging themselves in front of one of the two windows and pretending to be overwhelmed with the beauty and magnificence of the goods displayed.

"What beautiful soap," exclaimed Tom. "I never saw such beautiful soap, fellows. Pink and green and white! Looks almost good enough to wash with, doesn't it?"

"And get on to the lovely toilet set in the green velvet box," begged Tim awedly. "Scissors and brushes and little do-funnies and——"

"I'm going to buy a bottle of that hair-grower," announced Don. "I want to raise a beard."

"Let's get a bottle and present it to Uncle Sim," suggested Clint. Uncle Sim was Mr. Simkins, the Greek and Latin instructor, and was noticeably bald. The others chuckled and thought very well of the suggestion until Tom discovered that the price, as stated on the label, was one whole dollar. They had, they decided, better uses for what little money they carried. Eventually they went inside, and sat on stools in front of the small soda fountain and drank gaily-coloured concoctions which, according to Tim, later, sounded better than they tasted. Having exhausted the amusement to be derived from the drug store, they went to the fire house next door and, pressing their noses against the glass, debated what would happen if an alarm was rung in. There was a box beside the doors, a most tempting red box and Tim eyed it longingly until Don led him gently but firmly away from temptation.

In the small store across the street they examined all the

books and magazines displayed on the counters, which didn't take long, as literature was not a large part of the stock. Tim spent ten cents for a football guide, explaining that he had always wanted to know some of the rules of that game! Don bought some candy and Clint a bag of peanuts, although the others protested that if they ate truck they'd spoil their appetites for real food. The force of the protest was somewhat marred by the actions of the protestants, who helped themselves liberally to the contents of the two bags.

There was a convenient fence a few steps along the street and they perched themselves on the top rail and consumed the peanuts and candy and watched the "rush of the great city," to again quote the poetic Tim. During the next twenty minutes exactly eight carriages and four automobiles entered their range of vision; and at that Clint insisted that they had counted one automobile twice. He accused it of going around the block in order to add to the confusion. Possibly some three dozen people passed within sight, although that may have been a too liberal estimate. Tom at last declared that he couldn't stand the excitement any longer; that his brain reeled and his eyes ached; and that he was going to find a quiet spot far from the dizzy whirl. So they adjourned to the grocery and butcher shop and talked learnedly of loins and shoulders and ribs. And Clint dragged what he alluded to as a "brisket" into the conversation to the confusion of the others, who had never heard of it and didn't believe in it anyway. Tom said Clint meant "biscuit" and that this wasn't a bakery. Then he caught sight of some rather pathetic and unseasonable radishes and, having a passion for radishes, went in and purchased four bunches. That outlay led to an expenditure for salt, and as a large, round pasteboard carton of it was the least they could buy, they retreated down the street to the Inn porch, trickled the salt along the top of the railing, drew up chairs and consumed the radishes at their leisure. All, that is, save Tim. Tim didn't like radishes, called them "fire-crackers" and pretended to be deeply disgusted with his companions for eating them.

When the radishes were consumed they invaded the Inn and assaulted the water tank in force. Then, as there were practically no sights left to be viewed, they went back to their chairs and, as Tom had it, waited for inspiration. Don was for trolleying over to the shore, having a dip in the ocean and returning to school in good time. But Tim pointed out that the trolley line was a good half-mile distant, that he had not filled himself with radishes and was consequently quite famished for food and favoured remaining within easy distance of the Inn so that, in case he grew faint, he could reach sustenance. Don's motion was defeated. In view of what eventually occurred, that was, perhaps, unfortunate.

CHAPTER VII
FIGHTING FIRE

"THIS," said Tim presently, "is a bit dull, if you ask me. I came out for some excitement. Let's do something."

"What?" asked Clint, yawning loudly.

"Let's eat."

The others groaned.

"That's all right for you chaps, but I'm getting hungry," Tim asserted. "I thought we were going to have a feed. They'll be closing this place up the first thing we know. How about a rarebit, fellows?"

"Oh, let's wait awhile," said Don. "Let's take a walk and get up an appetite."

"Walk!" jeered Tim. "Gee, I've walked enough. And there's nothing the matter with my appetite right now. Tell you what——" Tim paused. An automobile was stopping in front of the Inn. The headlights suddenly dimmed and the single occupant, a tall man in a light overcoat, got out, walked up the path, ascended the steps and passed into the house. "Now, who's he?" asked Tim. "Say, I wish he'd loan us his car for awhile."

"Run in and ask him," suggested Tom. "He looked kind."

"Maybe he'd give us a ride if we asked him," pursued Tim. "It's a peach of a car; foreign, I guess."

"It's a Mercy Dear," said Tom.

"Or a Fierce Sorrow," hazarded Clint.

"Bet you it's a Cheerless," said Don, "or a Backhard."

"Don't care what it is," persisted Tim. "I want a ride in it."

"Let's go down and stand around it with our fingers in our mouths," said Tom, with a chuckle. "Perhaps he will take pity on us and ask us in."

"Or we might open the door for him," offered Don.

At that moment Clint, who had left his chair to lean across the railing and gaze past the end of the porch, interrupted with an exclamation. "Say, fellows, what's that light over there?" he asked eagerly.

"Fire, by jingo!" cried Tim.

"That's what!" agreed Tom. "Say, you don't suppose it's the school, do you?"

"Of course not! The school's over that way. Besides, that fire's away off; maybe two miles. Come on!" And Clint started for the steps.

"Wait!" called Tim. "I want to see the engine come out. Bet you it's a fine sight! Anyway, we can't foot it two miles."

"Maybe it isn't that far," said Don. "Fires look further than they are sometimes."

"Yes, and nearer, too," replied Tim. "Think we ought to run over and tell them about it?"

But that question was speedily answered by the sudden clanging of a gong inside the fire house, followed by the sound of running footsteps and, an instant later, the wild alarm of the shrill-tongued bell in the little belfry.

"My word!" exclaimed Tom. "I didn't know there were so many folks in the town!" Already a small-sized crowd had gathered in front of the fire house, some fifty yards up the street. The doors rolled open and a figure pushed through the throng and loped across the street and disappeared. The bell clanged on and on. Don and Clint and Tom made a dash for the steps. Tim slid over the railing. But before any of them had more than reached the sidewalk the tall owner of the automobile catapulted himself down the steps, hailing them as he came.

"Where is it, boys?" he shouted.

"Over there," answered Clint, pointing. But the glow in the sky was scarcely visible from the sidewalk and they all swarmed back to the porch again.

"I see," said the man. "Some farm house, I guess. They'll know at the fire house." He sprang down the steps again, the boys streaming after him. He was already in the car when Tim asked breathlessly: "You going, sir?"

"Sure! Want to come? Pile in, then. There are some packages in there. Look out for them."

Clint had already put his foot down hard on something that, whatever it might be, was never meant to be walked on, but he made no mention of the fact. The car leaped forward, swung to the right, stopped with a jerk six inches from a lamp-post, backed, straightened out and careened along to the fire house. All was excitement there. Men were rushing into the building and rushing out again, agitatedly donning rubber coats and hats. Speculation was rife. A score of voices argued as to the location of the fire. The throng swayed back and forth. The man in the car demanded information as he drew up at the curb and a dozen answers were flung at him. Then a small, fat man ran up and leaned excitedly across the front of the auto. "Hello, Mr. Brady!" he panted. "You going out there?"

"Yes, but I've got a load, Johnson. Where is it?"

"Don't no one seem to know. Jim Cogswell knows, but he's gone for the horses."

"Look out! Here they come!" "Get that auto out of the way there!" "Stand aside, everyone!" "Get a move on, Jim!" A lean little man in his shirt sleeves suddenly appeared leading two jogging horses, while a third horse trotted along behind. The crowd scampered aside and the horses beat a tattoo on the floor as they wheeled to their places. Mr. Brady jumped from his seat, pushed his way through the crowd as it closed in again about the doorway and disappeared. Tim whooped with delight.

"What did I tell you?" he demanded. "Didn't I say it would be a great sight? Gee, I haven't had such a good time since I had the measles!"

Mr. Brady reappeared, scrambled back to his seat and slammed the door behind him. "Jim says it's Corrigan's barn," he said. "Sit tight, boys!" The car leaped forward once more, took the first corner at twenty miles an hour, took the next at thirty and then, in the middle of a firm, hard road, simply roared away into the starlit darkness, the headlights throwing a great white radiance ahead. Tim, on the front seat, whipped off his cap and stuffed it into his pocket. Behind, the three boys huddled themselves low in the wide seat while the wind tore past them.

"Must be going ninety miles an hour!" gasped Clint.

"Suppose we bust something!" said Tom awedly.

Don braced his feet against the foot-rail. "Let it bust!" he answered exultantly.

That was a memorable ride. Tim owned afterward that he thought he had ridden fast once or twice before, but that he was mistaken. "I watched that speedometer from the time we turned the second corner," he declared, "and it never showed less than fifty-three and was generally around sixty! If I hadn't been so excited I'd been scared to death!"

Now and then one of the boys behind looked back along the road, but if anyone was following them the fact wasn't apparent. Almost before they were conscious of having travelled any distance the car topped a slight hill at a dizzy speed and the conflagration was in sight. A quarter of a mile distant a big barn was burning merrily. The car slowed down at the foot of the descent, swung into a lane and pitched and careened toward the burning structure. Other buildings were clustered about the barn and a good-sized white dwelling house stood in dangerous proximity. Between house and barn, standing out black against the orange glow of the fire, was a group of women and children, while a few men, not more than a half-dozen it seemed, were wandering hither and thither in the radiance. A horse with trailing halter snorted and dashed to safety as the automobile turned from the lane and came to a stop under an apple tree.

"Far as we go!" shouted Mr. Brady. "Come on, boys, and lend a hand!"

The lights dimmed, the engine stopped and the occupants of the car scrambled out and ran up the lane. "They can't save that barn," panted Mr. Brady, "but they'd ought to save the rest of them."

A man attired principally in a pair of overalls and a flannel shirt and carrying an empty bucket advanced to meet them.

"Is the engine coming?" he asked listlessly.

"They hadn't started when I left," answered Mr. Brady, "and I guess you needn't look for them for fifteen or twenty minutes. Got any water handy when it does come?"

"I've got a tank full up there, and there's a pond behind the house. But I don't know's they can do anything. Looks to me like everything's bound to go. Well, I got insurance."

"Got plenty of buckets?" asked Mr. Brady, peeling off his coat. "How many men are here?"

"About six or seven, I guess. Yes, there's buckets enough, but the heat's so fierce——"

"Animals all out?"

"There's some pigs down there. We tried to chase 'em out, but the plaguy things wouldn't go. We got the horses and cows out and a couple o' wagons. All my hay's done for, though. And there's a heap o' machinery in there——"

"Well, we can save the other buildings, can't we?" asked Mr. Brady impatiently. "Get your buckets and your men together, Corrigan. Here are five of us, and we can make a line and keep the roofs wet down until the engine comes, I guess. Send the women for all the pails and things you've got. Get a hustle on, man!"

Mr. Corrigan hesitated a moment and then trotted away. The water supply was contained in a wooden tank set some ten feet above ground, and high beyond that, dimly discernible through the cloud of smoke, the spectral arms of a wind-mill revolved imperturbably. Mr. Brady, followed by the boys, went on around to the further side of the burning building. It was a huge hip-roofed

36

structure. One end, that nearest the house, was already falling, and the tons of crackling hay in the mows glowed like a furnace. The heat, even at the foot of the wind-mill, a hundred feet or more away, was almost intolerable. A row of one-story buildings ran along one side of the barn, so near that the flying sparks blew over rather than on to them. Several other detached structures stood at greater distances. Mr. Brady, surveying the scene, shook his head doubtfully.

"Guess he's right," he said. "There's not much use trying to save those nearer buildings. We couldn't stay on those roofs a minute. I guess the chief danger will be from sparks lighting on the house and that creamery there. Things are mighty dry."

Four or five men dangling empty buckets, one of them Mr. Corrigan's son and the others neighbours, came up and asked about the fire department and Mr. Brady repeated what he had told the older man. "What we've got to do," he continued, "is to keep the roof on the house and the dairy wet. Those sparks are flying all over them. What's that small building over there?"

"That's the ice-house, Mr. Brady."

"Well, we won't bother about that. How many are there of us?"

"Six, I guess," said one of the men, but another corrected him.

"Old Man Meredith and Tom Young just drove in," he announced. "That makes eight of us, and there's five of you——"

"Well, come on, then," Mr. Brady interrupted briskly. "You fellows get your pails full and look after the dairy. Get on the roof, a couple of you, and keep it wet down. The rest can lug water. Got a ladder handy? All right. Somebody fetch it in a hurry. Hold on! Isn't there water in the dairy?"

"Yes, sir, plenty of it."

"Then fill your buckets inside and hand them up to the men on the roof. I'll take my gang and go over to the house."

The following half-hour was a busy time for the four boys. Mr. Brady and Don stood precariously athwart the ridge of the house roof while Tim and Clint and Tom, later assisted by others, filled buckets in the kitchen, raced up two flights of stairs and a short ladder—often losing half of their burden on the way—and passed them through a skylight to those outside. A dozen times the dry shingles caught fire under the rain of sparks, but Mr. Brady, climbing along the ridge like a cat, tossing buckets of water with unerring precision, kept the fire at bay. It was warm work for all. On the roof the heat of the fire was unpleasantly apparent, while in the house it was stiflingly close and the work of carrying the pails up and down stairs soon had the three boys in a fine perspiration and badly off for breath!

When the engines arrived, heralded by loud acclaim from the onlookers, who had by then multiplied remarkably, the barn was merely a huge pyre of glowing hay and burning timbers, only one far corner remaining erect. The piggery and adjoining buildings were ablaze in several places. The creamery roof had caught once or twice, but each time the flames had been subdued. If the engine and hose-cart and two carriages bearing members of the volunteer fire department had been slow in arriving, at least the fire-fighters got to work expeditiously and with surprisingly little confusion. Don, pausing for a moment in his labour of passing buckets to look down, decided that Brimfield had no cause to be ashamed of its department. In a jiffy the hose-cart was rattling across the yard— and, incidentally, some flower beds—in the direction of the pond behind the house, and a moment or two later the engine was pumping vigorously and a fine stream of water was wetting down the roofs of the threatened structures. Axes bit into charring timbers, sparks flew, enthusiastic, rubber-clad firemen dashed here and there, shouting loudly, the audience cheered and the worst was over!

With the collapse of the remaining section of barn wall the danger from sparks was past, and, emptying one final bucket, Mr. Brady, followed by a very wet, very tired and very warm Don, crept back through the skylight and joined the others below. Mr. Brady rescued his coat, led the way to the kitchen pump and drank long and copiously, setting an example enthusiastically emulated by the boys. Tim declared that if he drank as much as he wanted there wouldn't be enough water left to put out the fire with!

"Well, boys," said Mr. Brady, finally setting down the dipper and drawing a long breath, "I guess we did pretty well for amateurs, eh? I don't know whether we get any thanks, for I've a suspicion that Corrigan would have been just as pleased if everything had gone. From the way he talked when we got here I guess he wanted the insurance more'n he did the buildings!" Mr. Brady chuckled. "Well, we put one over on him in that case, eh? Want to stick around much longer? I guess most of the fun's over; unless they're going to serve some of that roast pig!"

"They got the pigs out," chuckled Tim. "They were running around here awhile ago like crazy. About twenty of them, big and little, squealing and getting between people's feet. Those pigs had the time of their lives!"

38

"Well, then, suppose we start along home?" said Mr. Brady. "You fellows ready?"

They agreed that they were. The remains of the barn were already blackening, and, while the firemen, evidently determined to make the most of the occasion, were still swinging axes and pouring water on the already extinguished and well-soaked buildings, there was no danger of further trouble. Mr. Corrigan, surrounded by a group of sympathetic neighbours, was cataloguing his losses and Mr. Brady called to him as they passed.

"Good-night, Corrigan! Sorry for you, but you've saved your house anyway!"

"Yes, sir, Mr. Brady. I'm greatly obliged to you, sir, and them young fellers, too. It's a bit of a loss, sir, but there's pretty good insurance."

"That's fortunate. Good-night!" Mr. Brady chuckled as they went on into the darkness of the orchard. "Bet you he's downright peeved with us, boys, for wetting that roof down! I happen to know that he's been losing money on this place for five years and been trying to sell it for a twelvemonth."

"You don't suppose," began Tom, "that he—er—that he——"

"Set the fire? Well, I'd rather not suppose about that. As there's no evidence against him we'd better give him the benefit of the doubt, I guess."

CHAPTER VIII
COACHING THE TACKLES

THE ride back was far less exciting. Mr. Brady drove the big car leisurely and conversed with Clint, who had succeeded to the seat of honour in front. Mr. Brady, it appeared, had a poultry farm some distance on the other side of Brimfield. He seemed a trifle surprised and pained when he discovered that Clint had never heard of the Cedar Ridge Poultry Farm, and at once issued an invitation to visit it.

"You come over some time and I'll show you some stock that'll open your eyes. Bring your friends along. Tell the conductor on the trolley where you want to go and he'll set you down right at my gate. You can't miss it, though, anyhow, for I've got nearly a quarter of a mile of houses there. Silver Campines are my specialty. Raise a few

White Wyandottes, too. You wouldn't think to look at me that the doctors came mighty near giving me up ten or eleven years ago, eh? Did, though. That was just after I finished college. They said the only thing would save me was hiking out to Colorado or Arizona or New Mexico. Some said one place and some said another. Seeing that they couldn't decide, I settled the question myself. Came out here, bought ten acres of land—I've got nearly forty now—and lived in a tent one Summer while my house was building. Doctors said it wouldn't do, but I fooled them. Slept out of doors every night, worked like a slave fourteen hours a day and put on flesh right from the start. I'm not what you'd call fat now, I guess, but you ought to have seen me then! An old chap I had putting up my first chicken house told me he could work me in nicely for a roosting pole! Went back to one of the doctors three years ago and had him look me over. He had to admit that I was a pretty healthy specimen. You could see that he was downright peeved about it, though!" Mr. Brady chuckled. "Then I settled the matter to my own satisfaction by taking out some life insurance. When I got my policy I stopped worrying about my health. You drop over some afternoon and let me show you how to live like a white man and make a little money, too. There's no life like it, and I wouldn't go back to the city if they gave me the Ritz-Carlton to live in!"

Clint responded that he and the others would like very much to visit Cedar Ridge some day, but that just now they were all pretty busy in the afternoons with football. That struck a responsive chord and Mr. Brady harked back to his school and college days when he, too, had fondled the pigskin. "I wasn't much of a player, though," he acknowledged. "I was sort of tall and puny-looking and not very strong. Still, I did get into my school team in my senior year and played on my freshman team in college. The next year I had to give it up, though. I'd like to come over some day and see you fellows play. I've always been intending to. I haven't seen a real smashing football game for years. That's funny, too, for I can remember the time when I used to think that if I could get on my 'varsity eleven I'd die happy." He laughed as he swept the searchlights around a corner. "A man's ambitions change, don't they? Now what I want to do is to raise the champion egg producer. I'm going to do it, too, before long."

And Clint quite believed it. Any man, he told himself, who could take command of a situation as Mr. Brady had that evening, and who could make enough money in the poultry business to own a three-thousand dollar automobile was capable of anything!

When they approached the town Mr. Brady swung off to the

left, explaining that he would take the boys up to the school. There was a moment of silence and then Clint protested weakly. "Shucks," was the reply, "it won't take five minutes longer, and after the way you fellows have worked tonight you don't deserve to have to walk home!"

"Well, then—then I guess you'd better let us out at the corner," said Tim. "We'd hate to wake up the masters, Mr. Brady."

"Oh, that's it, eh?" Mr. Brady laughed loudly. "Stayed out too late, have you?"

"I'm afraid we have, sir," said Clint. "We're supposed to be in hall before ten and it's long after that now. If you'll let us out at the corner of the grounds we can sort of sneak around back and maybe get in without being seen. Faculty's beastly strict about outstaying leave."

The car crossed the railroad track and presently pulled up quietly in the gloom of the trees along the road and the four boys noiselessly descended, shook hands, promised to pay a visit some day to Cedar Ridge and stole off to the right through the darkness. A moment later the tiny red light of the automobile vanished from sight. Tim called a halt at the wall. "You'd better bunk out with us tonight, Clint," he whispered. "We'll beat it around back of the gym and get in the shadows of the buildings. Say, Don, you're sure we left that window unlatched?"

"Of course we did! It hasn't been closed for a week."

"Then forward, my brave comrades! If anyone sees us we'd better scatter and hide out for awhile."

They climbed over a stone wall and made their way through a grove adjoining the school grounds, keeping close to the boundary fence. It was as dark as pitch in the woods and every now and then one or another would walk into a tree or fall over a root. Don's teeth were chattering like castanets, for the night had grown cooler and a little breeze was blowing from the west, and his clothing was still far from dry. They crept past the back of the Cottage very cautiously, for there were lights upstairs and down, and breathed easier when the black bulk of the gymnasium loomed before them and they could crawl over the fence and drop back into school ground. From the corner of the gymnasium to Billings was a long distance, and looked just now longer than it ever had before. Also, in spite of the fact that there was no moon, the night was surprisingly light and Tim scowled disapprovingly at the stars as they paused for an instant at the corner of the building to get their breaths.

"Keep low," advised Tim, "and make for Torrence. Then we'll

stay close to the walls of the buildings. You want to see if there's a window open in Torrence, Clint?"

"No, I'll stay with you fellows. I'd probably walk into a chair or a table and someone would take me for a burglar."

"Come on, then. Haste to yon enfolding darkness!"

They "hasted," and a second or two after were creeping, doubled up lest their heads show above the darkened windows and arouse unwelcome curiosity, along the rear of Torrence. Then they raced across the space dividing Torrence from Main Hall and repeated the proceedings until, finally, they were under the windows of Number 6 Billings. Both were open at the bottom and their doubts and tribulations were at an end. Clint was assisted in first, Tom followed and then Tim and, finally, Don was unceremoniously yanked up and through.

"Eureka!" breathed Tim. "Can you make it to your room, Tom? If you don't want to risk it you can bunk out here on the window-seat or somewhere."

"You may have half of my bed," offered Don. But Tom was already removing his shoes.

"If Horace hears me," he whispered, "he's got better ears than I think he has. Good-night, fellows. We had a bully time, even if we didn't get that rarebit!"

Tim groaned hollowly. "There! Now you've gone and reminded me that I'm starved to death!"

"Shut up," warned Don. "Don't forget that Horace's bedroom is right there." He nodded toward the wall. "Beat it, Tom, and don't fall over your feet!"

The door opened soundlessly, closed again and Tom was gone. They listened, and, although the transom was slightly open, not a creak or a shuffle reached them. "He's all right," whispered Tim. "Me for bed, fellows. Want to come in with me, Clint, or will you luxuriate on the window-seat?"

"Window-seat, thanks. Got a coat or something?"

Tim pulled a comforter from the closet shelf and tossed it to him, and quietly and quickly they got out of their clothes and sought their couches. Ten minutes later three very healthy snores alone disturbed the silence of Number 6.

The next morning Clint joined the others and walked unobtrusively along the Row with them in the direction of Wendell and breakfast, but when he reached Torrence he quite as unobtrusively slipped through the doorway and sought his room to repair his appearance and relieve the anxiety of Amory Byrd. And that seemed to conclude the adventure for all hands, and Don, for one, was extremely thankful that they had escaped detection and the punishment which would have certainly followed. But that Sunday afternoon, while on his way to Torrence to recover a book which Leroy Draper had borrowed in the Spring and neglected to return, he fell in with Harry Walton and made the disconcerting discovery that he had congratulated himself too soon. Don had no particular liking for Walton, although he by no means held him in the disdain that Amy Byrd and some others did, and he was a little surprised when Harry fell into step beside him.

"Have a good time last night?" asked Harry with an ingratiating leer.

"Last night?" echoed Don vacantly. He remembered then that Lawton roomed in Number 20 Billings, directly above Number 6. "What about last night?"

Harry winked meaningly and chuckled. "Well, I guess there was a party, wasn't there? I noticed you got home sort of late."

"Did I? What makes you think that?"

"I happened to be looking out my window, Don. It was sort of hot and I wasn't sleepy. Who were the other fellows?"

"Other fellows? I guess you didn't see any others, Walton."

Harry's saturnine countenance again wreathed itself with a growing grin. "Didn't, eh? All right. I probably imagined them."

"Maybe you were asleep and dreamed it," said Don gravely. "Guess you must have, Walton."

"Oh, I'm not going to talk, Don. You needn't be afraid of that."

"I'm not," responded the other drily. "Well, I'm going in here. So long, Walton."

"Bye, Don. I'm mum."

Don nodded and entered Torrence, but on the way upstairs he frowned disgustedly. He didn't believe for an instant that Walton would deliberately get them into trouble, but he might talk so much that the facts would eventually work around to one of the masters. Don wished that almost any fellow he knew save Walton had witnessed that entry by the window of Number 6. Later, when he returned from his visit to Roy Draper, without the book, by the way, since it had mysteriously disappeared, he recounted his conversation with Walton to Tim. Tim didn't let it bother him any, however.

"Harry won't give us away. Why should he? Besides, if he did he would know mighty well that I'd spoil his brunette beauty!"

"Well, he may tell it around and Horace or somebody'll hear it. That's all I'm worrying about."

43

"Don't worry, Donald. Keep a clear conscience and you'll never know what worry is. That's my philosophy."

Don smiled and dismissed the matter from consideration.

On Monday he had his first try at coaching the second team tackles and found that, after all, he got on fairly well. There were four candidates for the positions and two of them, Kirkwell and Merton, promised well. Kirkwell, in fact, had already had a full season of experience on the second. Merton was a graduate from his last year's hall team. The other two, Brace and Goodhugh, were novices and had everything to learn, and it was with them that Don laboured the hardest. Monday's practice ended with a ten-minute scrimmage between two hastily selected teams, and Don, for the first time that fall, played in his old position of left guard. Merton, who opposed him, found that he still had much to learn.

On Tuesday, after a long and grilling tackling practice at the dummy, Coach Boutelle announced his line-up for the scrimmage against the first team, and Don was disappointed to find that Kirkwell and not he was down for left guard. The right guard position went to Merton. Don, with Mr. Boutelle and a half-dozen of the more promising substitutes, followed their team about the field, Boots criticising and driving and Don breaking in with hurried instructions to the guards. The first team had no trouble in piling up four touchdowns that afternoon, even though three regulars were still out of the line-up. Between the short periods Don coached Kirkwell and Merton again, and Kirkwell, who was a decent chap but fancied himself a bit, was inclined to resent it.

"Chop it off, Gilbert," he said finally. "Give a fellow a chance to use his own brains a little. I'm no greenhorn, you know. I played guard all last year on this team."

"I know you did," answered Don. "And I don't say you can't play your position all right. But the best of us make mistakes, and Boots has told me to look out for them and try and correct them. I'd a lot rather be playing than doing this, Kirkwell, but while I am doing it I'm going to do it the best I know how. A fellow who isn't in the game sees a lot the player doesn't, and when——"

"Oh, all right. Only don't tell me stuff I know as well as I know my name, Gilbert. Don't nag."

"Sorry. I'll try not to. But you see what I mean about that stiff-arm business, don't you? Don't get out of position when you're not sure where the play's coming, Kirkwell. Stiff-arm your man and hold him off until you see what's doing. Then you can play him right or left or shove him back. Once or twice you waited too long to find out where the play was coming and you didn't hold your man off. Get me?"

"Yes, but we don't all play the position the same way, you know. What's the good of sparring with your man when you've got to find where the play's coming? You can't watch the ball and your opponent too, can you?"

"It doesn't sound reasonable," said Don, "but you can! You watch Hall do it, if you don't believe me. Maybe you don't actually look two ways at once, Kirkwell, but you can watch your man and locate the play at the same time. I suppose it comes with practice."

"I'd like to see you do it," replied Kirkwell aggrievedly.

"Watch Hall do it. He's the best guard around here. I'm not setting up as an example."

"You talk like it," muttered Kirkwell. But Merton, who had been a silent audience, stepped in to Don's support.

"Gilbert's only trying to help us, Ned. Quit grousing. Come on; time's up."

In spite of mutinous objections Kirkwell profited by Don's advice and instruction and soon showed an improvement in his defensive playing. It didn't appear that day, for Kirkwell was replaced by Don before the second period was more than a few minutes old, while Merton gave way to Goodhugh. Don's advent considerably strengthened the left of the second team's line and more than once during his brief presence there he had the satisfaction of outwitting Tom Hall and once got clear through and smeared a play well behind the first team's line.

Boots cut his squad from day to day and on Friday only some eighteen candidates remained. Brace went with the discard. Between parting with Brace and Goodhugh, Don, when consulted, chose to sacrifice the former. Possibly young Brace suspected Don's part in his release, for, for some time after that, he viewed Don with scowls.

Don's hand was now entirely healed, although the scars still showed, and, according to the doctor, would continue to show for a long time. Mr. Boutelle used Don at right guard during some portion of every scrimmage game against the first, a fact which caused Kirkwell a deal of anxiety. Kirkwell had from the first, and not unreasonably, resented Don's appearance with the second team squad. Don had been, as every fellow knew, slated for the first team, and Kirkwell thought it was unfair of him to drop back to the second and "try to do him out of his place." Feeling as he did, it isn't surprising that he took more and more unkindly to Don's teaching. It took all of Don's good nature at times to prevent an open break with Kirkwell. Once the latter accused Don of trying to "ball him up" so that he would play poorly and Don would get the position. The next day, though, he made an awkward apology for that accusation and was quite receptive to Don's criticisms and instructions. But Don's task was no easy one and it grew harder as the season progressed and the second team, especially as to its linemen, failed to develop the ability Mr. Boutelle looked for. Don more than once was on the point of resigning his somewhat thankless task, but Tim refused to sanction it, and what Tim said had a good deal of influence with Don.

"Well, then," he said moodily, "I hope Kirkwell will break something and get out of it."

"Tut, tut," remonstrated Tim. "Them's no Christian sentiments."

"I do, though. Or, anyway, I hope something will happen to let me out of it. Boots said he was afraid Robey would take me on the first, but I don't see any chance of it."

"I don't see why he doesn't, though," mused Tim. "Your hand's all right now and you're playing a corking good game. You can work all around any guard he's got except, maybe, Tom. Tom's rather a bit above the average, if you ask me. Neither Walton nor Pryme amounts to a whole lot."

"Robey's been playing Walton a good deal lately," said Don. "I wouldn't be surprised if he put him in ahead of Gafferty before long."

"There isn't a lot to choose between them, I guess," answered Tim. "Gafferty's no earthly good on offence. Wait till we run up against Benton tomorrow. Those huskies will show Gafferty up finely. And maybe some more of us," Tim added with a chuckle.

"Oh, well——" began Don, vaguely, after a minute.

But Tim interrupted. "Know what I think? I think Robey means to take you on the first later and is letting you stay with Boots just so you'll get fined down and speeded up a bit. You know you're still a little slow, Donald."

"I am?" Don asked in genuine surprise. "I didn't know it. How do you mean, slow, Tim?"

Tim leaned back in his chair and laced his fingers together behind his head. "Every way, Donald. I'm telling you this for your own good, dearie. I thought you realised it, though, or I'd have said it before. You start slow and you don't get up steam until the play's about over. If it wasn't that you're an indecently strong chap we'd get the jump on you every time. We do, as it is, only it doesn't do us much good, because you're a tough chap to move. Now you think it

46

over, Don. See if you can't ginger up a bit. Bet you anything that when you do Robey'll have you yanked off that second team in no time at all!"

"I'm glad you told me," said Don, after a moment's consideration. "I thought I was doing pretty well this fall. I know well enough it was being all-fired slow that kept me off the first last fall, but I surely thought I'd picked up a whole lot of speed. I'll have to go back to practising starts, I guess."

"Oh, never mind the kindergarten stuff, old man. Just put more jump into it. You'll find you can do it all right, now that you know about it. Why, I'll bet you'll be performing like a Jack rabbit before the season's over!"

"Like a jackass, more likely," responded Don ruefully.

"No, for a jackass, dearie, doesn't take a hint."

"Well, but I don't believe I can play any faster, Tim. If I could I'd be doing it, wouldn't I? Just naturally, I mean."

"Never mind the conundrums, Don. You try it. If you do I'll be willing to guarantee you a place on the first."

"I guess your guarantee wouldn't cut much ice," objected Don, with a laugh. Then he sobered and added: "Funny game, though, me coaching Kirkwell and Merton and Goodhugh. Looks as if I was the one needed the coaching."

"Sure. We all need it. No one's perfect, Don, although, without boasting, I will say that I come pretty near it."

"You come pretty near being a perfect chump, if that's what you mean."

Tim shook his head. "It isn't at all what I mean. Now cut out the artless prattle and let me find some sense in this history stuff—if there is any!"

CHAPTER IX
THE WIDTH OF A FINGER

AT chapel the next morning Mr. Fernald, the principal, after the usual announcements had been made, lifted a newspaper from the table at his side and ran his eyes over an item there. "I have here," he said, "a copy of this week's Brimfield Times, which tells of an incident of which I had not learned. In telling of a fire on Saturday night last which destroyed a barn and damaged other buildings on the farm of Mr. William Corrigan, some three miles from the village, the Times makes mention of the valuable assistance of a Mr. Grover Brady and four boys of this school. According to the Times, Mr. Brady and four boys dashed to the scene in a high-powered automobile, organised a bucket brigade and saved"—Mr. Fernald consulted his authority again—"saved the dwelling house from the devouring element. The metaphor is that of the paper. Possibly the Times is misinformed with regard to the heroic young firemen, although I hope not. I should be very pleased to discover that they were really Brimfieldians. If they were, if they are before me at this moment, I trust they will signify the fact by standing up. I'm sure we'd all like to know their identity and give them well-deserved applause. Now then, will the modest heroes kindly reveal themselves?"

Silence ensued, a silence broken only by a few whispers and some shuffling of feet. Every fellow's eyes searched the room, or, at least, that is true of almost every fellow. Tim smiled innocently and expectantly at the principal, Clint studied the back of the head in front of him most interestedly, Don observed the scar in his hand absorbedly and Tom grinned because Steve Edwards was whispering from the side of his mouth: "Why don't you get up, you bloomin' hero, why don't you get up?" Harry Walton was smiling that knowing smile of his and doing his best to catch Don's eye. And Don somehow knew it and didn't dare look toward him.

"I'm disappointed," said Mr. Fernald after a minute. "Either the paper is mistaken or the fellows are over-modest. Well, if they won't speak for themselves perhaps someone else will volunteer to wrest them from the obscurity they so evidently court. How about that, boys? Anyone know who the heroes are?"

Again silence for an instant, and then, in various parts of the room, the sudden moving of seats or tramping of feet as though someone was about to get up. But no one did, and some of the younger boys in front began to titter nervously. Mr. Fernald smiled and laid the Brimfield Times back on the table.

"No heroes amongst us, eh? Well, doubtless if any of you had been there you'd have performed quite as well as these unknown young gentlemen did. I like to think so. Dismissed."

"Do you think he suspects us?" asked Tom as he ranged himself beside Tim on the way out. "Gee, I thought once he was looking right at me!"

"That's what it is to have a guilty conscience," replied Tim, in a virtuous tone. "Of course he doesn't suspect. If he did he'd have named us, sure as shooting. The funny part of it is that he hasn't thought about what time the fire was! Maybe the paper didn't say. If he knew that he'd probably be a sight more anxious to find us!"

"I was scared stiff that Harry Walton would blab. I didn't dare look at him."

"Harry doesn't know you were with us. He recognised Don, or says he did, and he naturally thinks I was along, but he doesn't know who the other two were. If he opens his mouth I'll brain him."

"I guess he won't. He's a sort of a pup, but he isn't mean enough for that. Gee, but it almost ruined my appetite for breakfast!"

"Even if Josh did find out," said Tim as they turned into Wendell, "he wouldn't do much to us, I guess. It wasn't our fault the fire was late in getting started, and the paper calls us heroes——"

"I don't believe it does. That's some of Josh's nonsense. I'm going to get a copy of the Times and see what it does say."

"Take my advice and let the Times alone," advised Tim. "Why, I wouldn't be seen with a copy of it in my possession! It would be circumstantial evidence, or corroborative evidence or something horrid, and I'd get pinched for sure. You keep away from the Times, dearie."

There was a good deal of interested speculation as to the identity of the four youths who had participated in the rescue of Farmer Corrigan's dwelling, but the general opinion was to the effect that the local paper had erred. One fellow made the suggestion in Don's hearing that if faculty would look it up and see who had leave of absence Saturday night they might spot the chaps. Don sincerely hoped the idea wouldn't occur to Mr. Fernald!

But interest in the matter soon waned, for Brimfield was to play Benton Military Academy that afternoon and what sort of a showing she would make against that very worthy opponent was a far more absorbing subject for speculation. Benton had been defeated handily enough last year, but reports from the military academy this Fall led Brimfield to expect a hard contest. And her expectations were fulfilled.

Benton brought at least a hundred neatly uniformed rooters along and the field took on a very gallant appearance. The visitors seemed gaily confident of victory and from the time they marched into the field and took their places in the stand until the kick-off there was no cessation of the songs and cheers from the blue-clad cohorts. Coach Robey started his best men in that game and, as was quickly proved, needed to. The first period was a bitterly contested punting duel in which Rollins, and, later, St. Clair came off second best. But the difference in the kicking of the rival teams was not

49

sufficient to allow of much advantage, and the first ten-minute set-to ended without a score. In fact, neither team had been at any time within scoring distance of the other's goal line. When play began again Benton changed her tactics and started a rushing game that for a few minutes made headway. But a fumble cost her the ball and a possible score on the Maroon-and-Grey's twenty-yard line and the latter adopted the enemy's plan and banged at the soldiers' line for fair gains. A forward pass brought the spectators to their feet and gained twenty-two yards for Brimfield, Steve Edwards being on the receiving end of a very pretty play. But Benton stiffened presently and Brimfield was forced to kick.

That kick spelled disaster for Brimfield. Rollins dropped back to near his own thirty yards and sent a remarkable corkscrew punt to Benton's twenty. It was one of the prettiest punts ever seen on the Brimfield gridiron, for it was so long that it went over the quarter-back's head, so high that it enabled the Maroon-and-Grey ends to get well down under it and was nicely placed in the left-hand corner of the field. The Benton quarter made no effort to touch it while it was bounding toward the goal line, for with both Edwards and Holt hovering about him a fumble might easily have resulted, and it was only when the pigskin had settled down to a slow, toppling roll and it was evident that it did not mean to go over the line that the Benton quarter seized it. What happened then was little short of a miracle. Both Captain Edwards and Holt took it for granted that the quarter-back meant to drop on the ball and call it down, and, since there was no necessity to smother the opponent, each waited for the other to tackle and hold him. But the first thing anyone knew the Benton quarter had the ball in his hands, had squirmed somehow between Edwards and Holt and was speeding up the middle of the field!

Between him and the fifty-yard line friend and foe were mingled, and to win through seemed a preposterous undertaking. And yet first one and then another of the enemy was passed, team-mates formed hasty interference for the runner and, suddenly, to the consternation of the Brimfield stand, the quarter, with the ball snuggled in the crook of his left elbow, was out of the mêlée, with a clear field before him and two Benton players guarding his rear. Crewe made a desperate effort to get him near the thirty-yard line, but the interference was too much for him, and after that, although Brimfield trailed the runner to the goal line and over, there was no doubt as to the result. And when the Benton quarter deposited the ball squarely between the posts and laid himself down beside it friend and foe alike arose from their seats and cheered him long and loudly. Never had a more spectacular run been made there, for not only had the quarter practically traversed the length of the field, but had eluded the entire opposing eleven.

Benton deserved to secure the odd point by kicking goal, but goal-kicking was the quarter-back's business and he was far too tuckered to try, and so the player who did make the attempt failed miserably, and Benton had to be satisfied with those six points. Probably she was, for she cheered madly and incessantly while the period lasted and then spent the half-time singing triumphant paeans. And those military academy chaps could sing, too! Brimfield, a bit chastened, listened and applauded generously and only found her own voice when the Maroon-and-Grey warriors trotted back again.

Carmine had given place to McPhee at quarter and Holt to Cheep at right end. Otherwise Brimfield's line was the same as in the first half. McPhee opened his bag of tricks soon after play began and double-passes and delayed-passes and a certain fake plunge at guard with quarter running wide outside the drawn-in end made good gains and took the ball down the field with only one halt to Benton's twenty-three yards. There the military academy team solved a fake-kick and St. Clair was laid low behind his line. Rollins made up the lost distance and a little more besides, and finally, with the ball on Benton's nineteen yards on fourth down, Captain Edwards called for a try-at-goal and Rollins dropped back to the thirty. Fortunately the Maroon-and-Grey forwards held back the plunging enemy in good style, Rollins had all the time he wanted, the pigskin dropped neatly over the bar, and the score-board figures proclaimed 6 to 3.

Benton kicked off and once more Brimfield started up the field, St. Clair, Tim Otis and Rollins banging the line from end to end and Edwards varying the monotony by sweeping around behind and launching himself off on wide runs. But the advance slackened near the middle of the field and an attempted forward pass was captured by Benton. That play brought the ten-minute period to an end.

Benton tried the Brimfield centre and got through for four yards, hit it again and made three and placed the ball on the home team's forty-yard line. Time was called for Brimfield and Danny Moore trotted on to administer to Gafferty. The left guard was soon on his feet again, although a trifle unsteady, it seemed, and Benton, with three yards to gain, swung into the other side and pushed a half-back through for the distance. Carmine replaced McPhee and Holt went back to end position. Benton once more thrust at Gafferty and, although the secondary defence plugged the hole, went through for two yards. Time was again called and this time the trainer led Joe Gafferty off the field, the latter protesting bitterly, and Harry Walton was hurried in. Benton tried a forward pass and made it go for a small gain and then, on third down, got past Thayer and reached the eighteen before Carmine tipped up the runner. Across the gridiron, Benton's supporters yelled mightily and a second touchdown looked imminent.

Benton fumbled and recovered for a two-yard loss and then sent that heroic quarter up the field to try a drop kick. It looked easy enough, for the ball was near the twenty-eight yards and in front of the right hand goal post. Captain Edwards implored his men to block the kick and comparative quiet fell over the field. Back shot the ball and the quarter's foot swung at it, but the left side of the Benton line crumbled and Hall and Crewe flung themselves into the path of the ball. Four seconds later it was snuggled under Tim Otis's chest near the thirty-five yards, for Tim had followed the forwards through and trailed the bouncing pigskin up the field.

That misadventure seemed to take the heart out of the visitors, and when Brimfield, with new courage and determination, smashed at her line she fell back time and again. Substitutes were sent in lavishly, but although the right side of the Benton line stiffened for awhile, the left continued weak. Coach Robey sent in Compton to replace Steve Edwards and, later, Howard for St. Clair. With the best part of five minutes left, Brimfield hoped to put over a winning touchdown, and the backs responded gallantly to Carmine's demands. Near the enemy's forty-yard line Rollins threw a neat forward to Holt and the latter raced along the side of the field for a dozen yards before he was forced over the line. That took the ball to Benton's twenty-one. Two tries at the line netted but six yards and Compton took the pigskin on an end-around play and just made the distance.

Brimfield hammered the enemy's left wing and reached her five-yard line in three downs, but Benton, fiercely determined, her feet on the last line mark, was putting up a strong defence. Tom Hall, captain pro tem., and Carmine consulted. A forward pass might succeed, and if it did would win the game, but Benton would be watching for it and neither Holt nor Compton was a brilliant catcher of thrown balls. A goal from the field would only tie the score, but it seemed the wisest play. So Rollins dropped back to the twenty and stretched his arms. But Benton was sure a forward was to result and when the ball went back her attempts to block the kick were not very enthusiastic. That was fortunate for Brimfield, for

Thursby's pass had been short and Rollins had to pick the ball from the turf before he could swing at it. That delay was almost his undoing, since the Benton forwards were now trickling through, and it was only by the veriest good fortune that the ball shot between them from Rollins's toe and, after showing an inclination to pass to the left of the goal and changing its mind in mid-air, dropped over the bar barely inside the post. Brimfield cheered and the 3 on the board changed to 6. Coach Robey called Rollins and Tim Otis out, replacing them with Martin and Gordon. Brimfield kicked off once more and, with a scant minute and a half to play, the Maroon-and-Grey tried valiantly to add another score.

Carmine caught on his twenty and took the ball to the thirty-six before he was stopped, and Brimfield cheered wildly and danced about in the stand. Plugging the line would never cover that distance to the farther goal line and so Carmine sent Gordon off around the left end. But Gordon couldn't find the hole and was run down for no gain. A forward pass, Carmine to Compton, laid the ball on the forty-eight yards. Howard slid off right tackle for six and, on a fake-kick play, Martin ran around left end for seven more. Brimfield shouted imploringly from the stand and, across the field, Benton cheered incessantly, doggedly, longing for the whistle.

The Benton team used all allowable methods to waste time. The timekeeper hovered nearby, his eyes darting from the galloping hand of his watch to the players. "Twenty-nine seconds," he responded to Tom Hall's question. Carmine clapped his hands impatiently.

"Signals now! Make this good! Left tackle over! 27—57—88—16! Hep! 27—57—88——"

The backs swung obliquely to the right, Carmine dropped from sight, his back to the line, Benton's left side was borne slowly away, fighting hard, and confusion reigned. Then Carmine whirled around, sprang, doubled over, through the scattered right side of the enemy's line, challenged only by the end, who made a desperate attempt at a tackle but failed, and, with only the opposing quarter between him and the goal line, raced like the wind. About him was a roaring babel of sound, voices urging him on, shouts of dismay, imploring shrieks from behind. Then the quarter was before him, crouching with out-reached hands, a strained, anxious look on his dirt-streaked face.

They met near the twenty-yard line. The Benton quarter launched himself forward. Carmine swung to the left and leaped. A hand groped at his ankle, caught, and Carmine fell sprawling to the turf. But he found his feet like a cat, wrenched the imprisoned ankle free and went staggering, stumbling on. Again he fell, on the five-yard line, and again the Benton quarter dived for him. But Carmine was not to be stopped with the line only five short yards away. He wrested himself to his feet again, the arms of the Benton quarter squirming about his knees, plunged on a stride, dragging the enemy with him, found his legs locked firmly now, struggled desperately and then flung himself sidewise toward the last white streak. And as he fell his hands, clasping the ball, reached forward and a whistle blew.

It was said afterward that a half-inch decided that touchdown. And the half-inch was on the wrong side of the line! Carmine wept frankly when he heard the decision and Tom Hall had to be held away from the referee, but facts were facts and Carmine had lost his touchdown and Brimfield the victory by the width of a finger!

Benton departed joyously, cheering and singing, and Brimfield tried hard to be satisfied with a drawn game. But she wasn't very successful, and for the next few days the referee's decision was discussed and derided and regretted.

What sorrow Don felt was largely mitigated when, after supper that evening, Steve Edwards found him in front of Billings. "You come to us Monday, Don," said the captain. "Robey told me to tell you. Joe Gafferty's got a rib caved in and is out of it for a fortnight at least. Get Tim to coach you up on the signals. Don't forget."

As though he was likely to!

CHAPTER X
TIM EXULTS AND EXPLAINS

WHEN Don told Tim the latter insisted on performing a triumphal dance about the room to the tune of "Boola." When Don squirmed himself loose Tim continued alone until the droplight was knocked to the floor at the cost of one green shade. Then he threw himself, panting but jubilant, on his bed and hilariously kicked his feet in air. Don observed him with a faint smile.

"You wooden Indian, you!" exclaimed Tim, sitting up and dropping his feet to the floor with a crash. "There you stand like a— a graven image, looking as though you'd just received an invitation to a funeral! Cheer, you idiot! Make a noise! Aren't you tickled to death?"

"You bet I am!" replied Don.

"Well, do something, then! You ought to have a little of my Latin temperament, Don. You'd be a heap easier to live with. If it was I who had just been waited on humbly by the first team captain and invited to join the eleven I'd—I'd make a—a noise!"

"What do you think you've been doing?" laughed Don. "You'll have Horace in here in a minute. Steve says you're to coach me on the signals."

"Tomorrow!" Tim waved his hand. "Time enough for that, Don. Just now it behooves us to celebrate."

"How?" asked Don.

Tim thought long and earnestly. Finally, "Let's borrow Larry Jones's accordion and serenade Josh!" he said.

"Let's not. And let's not go to a fire, either! Think of something better, Timmy."

"Then we'll go out and bay at the moon. I've got to do something! By the time Joe's got his busted rib mended you'll have that left guard position nailed to the planks, Don."

"How about Walton?" asked Don dubiously.

"A fig for Walton! Two figs for him! A whole box of figs! All you've got to do is speed up a bit and——"

"Suppose I can't?"

"Suppose nothing! You've got to! If you don't you'll have me to fight, Donald. If you don't cinch that position in just one week I—I'll take you over my knee and spank you with a belt! Come on over to Clint's room. Let us disseminate the glorious tidings. Let us——"

"I'd rather learn the signals," said Don. "There's only tonight and tomorrow, you know."

Tim appealed despairingly to the ceiling with wide-spread hands. "There's no poetry in his soul," he mourned, "no blood in his veins!" He faced Don scornfully. "Donald P. Gilbert is your name, my son, and the P stands for Practical. All right, then, draw up a chair and let's have it over. To think, though, that I should have to sit indoors a night like this and teach signals to a wooden-head! I wooden do it for anyone else. Ha! How's that! Get a pad and a pencil and try to look intelligent."

"All right? Mark 'em down, then. Starting at the left, number your holes 1, 3, 5, 7, 8, 6, 4, 2. Got that? Number your left end 1, the next man 3, the next 5. Omit centre. Right guard 6, right tackle 4, right end 2. Now, your backfield. Quarter 0, left half 7, right half 8, full-back 9."

"Gee, that's hard to remember," murmured Don.

"And hard to guess," answered Tim. "Now, your first number, unless it's under thirty, is a fake. If it's under thirty it means that the next number is the number of a play. Over thirty, it means nothing. Your second digit of your second number is your runner. The second digit of the third number is the hole. The fourth number, as you doubtless surmise, is also a fake. Now, then, sir! 65—47—23—98! What is it?"

"Left half between end and tackle."

"On the left. Correct. 19—87—77—29?"

"I don't know. Nineteen calls for a numbered play."

"Right again, Mr. Gilbert, your performance is startling! The pity of it is, though, that about the time you get these signals pat Robey'll change them for the Claflin game. So far we've only got eight numbered plays, and they aren't complicated. Want to go into them tonight?"

"No, I guess not. I'd rather get these holes and players sort of fixed in my mind first. We'll go over the plays tomorrow, if you don't mind."

"It will break my heart, but I'll do it for you. Now will you come over to Clint's?"

"I'd rather not, Tim. You go. I want to mull over these signals."

Presently, having exhausted his vocabulary on his room-mate, Tim went. Don settled his head in his hands and studied the numbered diagram for the better part of an hour. Don was slow at memorising, but what was once forced into his mind stayed there. A little before ten o'clock he slipped the diagram under a box in a bureau drawer and went to bed with a calm mind, and when Tim returned riotously a few minutes later Don was sleeping peacefully.

On Monday, in chapel, Don and the "heroes" of Farmer Corrigan's conflagration had another shock, and Don, for one, wondered when he was to hear the last of that affair. "Since last week," said Mr. Fernald drily, "when I requested the four boys who helped to put out a fire at the Corrigan farm to make themselves known to an admiring public, I have gained an understanding of their evident desire to conceal their identities. I am forced to the conclusion that it was not altogether modesty that kept them silent. The fire, it appears, did not break out until nearly half-past nine. Consequently the young gentlemen were engaged in their heroic endeavours at a time when they should have been in their dormitories. I have not yet found out who they were, but I am making earnest efforts to do so. Meanwhile, if they wish to lighten the consequences of their breach of school regulations, I'd earnestly advise them to call and see me. I may add that, in view of the unusual circumstances, had they made a clean breast of the affair I should have dealt very leniently with them. That is all, I think. Dismissed."

None of the culprits dared to so much as glance at the others on the way out of the hall, but afterward, when breakfast was over, they gathered anxiously together in Number 6 Billings and discussed the latest development with lowered voices, like a quartette of anarchists arranging a bomb party.

"He's right up on his ear," said Clint gloomily. "If he gets us now he will send us all packing, and don't you doubt it!"

"Piffle!" This from Tim, the least impressed of the four. "Probation is all we'd get. Didn't the paper say we were heroes?"

"No, it didn't," answered Tom shortly. "And I wish that paper was in Halifax!"

"Might as well be fired as put on pro," said Clint. "It would mean no more football this year for any of us. My word, wouldn't Robey be mad!"

"Wouldn't I be!" growled Tom. "Look here, do you really suppose he's trying to find out who we were, or was that just a bluff to scare us into 'fessing up!"

"Josh isn't much of a bluffer," observed Don judiciously. "What he says he means. What I don't savvy is why he hasn't found out already. Every hall master has a record of leaves."

"Yes, but it was Saturday night and I'll bet half the school had leave," said Tim. "I dare say, though, that if any fellows are suspected we're amongst 'em, Don. Being on the first floor, Josh knows we could sneak in easily. Still, he can't prove it on us."

"I'm not so sure," replied Don thoughtfully. "Suppose he asked Mr. Brady?"

A dismayed silence ensued until Tom laughed mirthlessly.

"That's one on us," he said. "We never thought of that. Maybe he has asked Brady already."

"Brady doesn't know our names," said Tim. "You didn't tell him, did you, Don?"

"No, he didn't ask. But he could easily describe us so that Josh would recognise us, I guess."

"That's the trouble with being so plaguy distinguished looking," mourned Tim. "Seems to me, fellows, that there's just one thing to be did, and did sudden."

"You mean warn Mr. Brady?" asked Clint.

"Exactly, my discerning young friend. Maybe the horse is stolen——"

"What horse?" asked Tom perplexedly.

"Merely a figure of speech, Tom. I was about to observe when so rudely interrupted——"

"Oh, cut out the verbiage," growled Tom.

"That possibly it was too late to lock the stable door," continued Tim, "but we'd better do it, just the same. Let's see if he has a telephone."

"Of course he has," said Clint, "but I don't think it would be safe to call him up. We'd better see him. Or write him a letter."

"He wouldn't get a letter until tomorrow, maybe," objected Don. "One of us had better beat it over to his place as soon as possible and ask him to keep mum."

"I can't go," said Tom. "I've got four recits this morning and Robey would never let me off practice."

"I don't believe any of us will do much work this afternoon," said Tim. "I'll go if Robey'll let me cut. I wish someone would come along, though. It's a dickens of a trip to make alone. You come, Clint."

"I will if I can. We'll ask Robey at dinner. What shall we say to this Brady man?"

"Just tell him what's doing and ask him to forget what we looked like if Josh writes to him or calls him up or anything. Brady's a good old scout, I'll bet," added Tim with conviction. "Maybe we'd better buy a setting of eggs to get on the good side of him."

"Don't be a chump," begged Tim. "I don't call this a comedy situation, if you do, Tim. I'd certainly hate to get on pro and have to drop football!"

"Don't be a chump," begged Tom. "I don't say it's a comedy, but there's no use weeping, is there? What's done is done, and we've got to make the best of it, and a laugh never hurt anyone yet."

"Well, then, let's make the best of it," answered Tom peevishly. "Talking doesn't do any good."

"Neither does grouching," said Tim sweetly. "You leave it all to Clint and me, Tom. We're a swell pair of fixers. If we can get to Brady before Josh does we're all right. And it's a safe wager Josh hasn't asked Brady yet, for if he had he'd be on to us. There's the nine o'clock bell, fellows, and I've got a recit. See you later. Hope for the best, Tom, and fear the worst!"

Tim seized his books and dashed out, followed more leisurely by Clint. Tom remained a few minutes longer and then he, too, took his departure, still filled with forebodings. Don, left to himself, drew a chair to the table and began to study. Truth, however, compels me to state that what he studied was not his German, although he had a recitation coming in forty minutes, but two sheets of buff paper torn from a scratch-pad and filled with writing interspersed with numerals and adorned with strange diagrams, in short, Tim's elucidation of the eight numbered plays which up to the present comprised Brimfield's budget of tricks. It can't be said that Don covered himself with glory in Mr. Daley's German class that morning or that the instructor was at all satisfied, but Don had the secret satisfaction of knowing that stored away in the back of his brain was a very thorough knowledge of the Brimfield football signal code and of Mr. Robey's special plays.

CHAPTER XI
MR. BRADY FORGETS

THAT afternoon Don's knowledge stood him in good stead, for with more than half the first-string players excused from practice, his services were called on at the start, and, with McPhee and Cotter running the squad, the signal drill was long and thorough. Harry Walton viewed Don's advent with disfavour. That was apparent to Don and anyone else who thought of the matter, although he pretended a good-natured indifference that wasn't at all deceiving. Don more than once caught his rival observing him with resentment and dislike, and, remembering that Harry Walton had been a witness of his unconventional return to hall that night, he experienced misgivings. Of course, Harry wouldn't "peach," but— well, Don again wished anyone rather than Harry had stumbled on the secret.

But he didn't have much time for worrying about that matter, for Coach Robey went after them hard that day. In the practice game with the second team Don started at left guard and played the position until within a few minutes of the whistle. Then Harry Walton, who had been disgruntledly adorning the bench, took his place. He didn't look at Don as he accepted the latter's head-guard, but Don was well aware that Harry felt anything but good-will for him. Naturally enough, Harry had, Don reflected, expected to step into Gafferty's place without opposition when news of the extent of the latter's injury had become known, and it was undoubtedly a big disappointment to him to discover that he had to fight a new opponent. Don could sympathise with Harry, for he had endured disappointments himself during his brief football career, but it is difficult to sympathise very enthusiastically when the subject of your sympathy shows his dislike for you, and Don metaphorically shrugged his shoulders as he trotted up to the gymnasium.

"It isn't my fault," he said to himself. "I didn't bust Joe Gafferty's rib and I'm not responsible for Robey's taking me on the first team. Walton will just have to make the best of it."

Don couldn't flatter himself that he had played that afternoon with especial brilliancy, although he had managed to hold his end up fairly well. The fact was that he had been so intent on getting speeded into his performance that he had rather skimped the niceties of line-play. And he wasn't at all certain that he had shown any more speed than usual, either. He awaited Mr. Robey's appearance in the locker-room with some apprehension, certain that if he had erred badly he would soon learn of it. When the coach did arrive at the tail of the procession of panting players and said his say without once singling out Don for special attention, the latter was relieved. He couldn't, he told himself, have done so very badly, after all!

Tom walked back to Billings with Don to learn the result of Tim's and Clint's embassy to the Cedar Ridge Poultry Farm, for the two had obtained leave of absence from Mr. Robey and had set forth on their journey the minute a three o'clock recitation was finished. Tim wasn't in Number 6 when they reached it, but he and Clint tramped in soon after, dusty and weary but evidently triumphant. Tim narrated their experiences.

"Missed the three-fifty car, just as I told Clint we would if he didn't hustle——"

"I had to find a cap to wear, didn't I?" interpolated Clint.

"Well, we found the place all right, fellows, and, say, it's some poultry farm, believe me, dearies! Isn't it corking, Clint?"

Clint grunted assent, stretching tired legs across the floor.

"There's about a thousand acres of it, I guess, and a mile of red chicken houses and runs, or whatever you call 'em. How many hens and things did he tell us he had, Clint?"

"Eighteen hundred, I think. Maybe it was eighteen thousand. I don't remember. All I know is there were chickens as far as you could see, and then some."

"Never mind the descriptive matter," urged Tom. "What did he say? Had Josh been at him? Did he promise——"

"I'm coming to that, dearie. When we found him he was doing

60

something to that car of his in a cute little garage. And, say, it's an eight-cylinder Lothrop, and a regular jim-dandy! Well, he took us into his house first——"

Tom groaned in despair.

"——And fed us on crackers and cake and ginger ale. Say, he's got a peach of a bungalow there; small but entire; and a cute little Jap who cooks and looks after things for him. Well, then he took us out and showed us around the place. Chickens! Gee, I didn't know there were so many in the world! And we saw the incubators and the—what you call them—brooders, and——"

"For the love of mud!" exclaimed Tom. "Can't you get down to dots? Is it all right or isn't it?"

Tim smiled exasperatingly. "Then he showed us——"

Tom arose to his feet and took a step toward him.

"It's all right," said Tim hurriedly. "Everything, Thomas! We told him what was up and how we didn't want Josh to find out it was us who attended Mr. Corrigan's fire party and asked him if he would please not remember what we looked like if Josh asked him. And he said——"

"He laughed," interrupted Clint, and chuckled himself.

"That's right! He laughed a lot. 'You're a little bit late,' he said. 'Mr. Fernald called me up by telephone nearly a week ago, fellows, and wanted to know all about it.' 'You didn't tell him?' I yelped. 'No, I couldn't,' he said. 'You see, you hadn't told me your names, and it was pretty dark that night and somehow or other I just couldn't seem to recall what you looked like! Mr. Fernald sounded considerably disappointed and like he didn't quite believe me, but that can't be helped.' Say, fellows, I wanted to hug him! Or—or buy an egg or something! Honest, I did! He's all right, what?"

"He's a corker!" said Tom, sighing with relief. "You don't suppose Corrigan or any of the others there that night would remember us, do you?"

"Not likely. Mr. Brady didn't think so, anyway."

"Then it's all to the merry!" cried Tom. "Gee, but that's a load off my mind!"

"Off your what?" asked Tim curiously.

"It's all right if Harry Walton keeps quiet," said Don. "If he gets to talking——"

"If he does I'll beat him up," said Tim earnestly. "But he won't. He wouldn't be such a snip, in the first place, and he wouldn't dare to in the second."

"N-no, I guess not," agreed Don. But his tone didn't hold much conviction. "Only, if——"

61

"I'll tell you fellows one thing," announced Tom vehemently.

"Don't strain yourself," advised Tim.

"And that," continued the other, scowling at the interruption, "is that no one gets me into any more scrapes until after the Claflin game!"

"Gee, to hear you talk," exclaimed Tim indignantly, "anyone would think we'd tied you up with a rope and forcibly abducted you! Who's idea was it, anyway, to go to the village that night?"

"Yours, if you want to know! I don't say I didn't go along willingly enough, Tim. What I do say is—never again! Anyway," he added, "not until football's over!"

Morgan's School, which had defeated Brimfield the year before, 6 to 3, came and departed. Brimfield took the visitor's measure this time, and, although she only scored one touchdown and failed to kick goal, the contest was far less close and interesting than the score would suggest. Brimfield played the opponents to a standstill in the first half and scored just before the end of it. In the third quarter Coach Robey began substituting and when the last ten minutes started the Maroon-and-Grey had only three first-string fellows in her line-up. The substitutes played good football and, while not able to push the pigskin across Morgan's line, twice reached her fifteen yards and twice tried and narrowly missed a goal from the field.

On the whole it could not be said that Brimfield's performance that blustery Saturday afternoon was impressive, for she was frequently caught napping on the defensive, showed periods of apathy and did more fumbling, none of which resulted disastrously, than she should have. Tim Otis had a remarkably good day and was undeniably the best man in the backfield for the home team. Carmine played a heady, snappy game, and Don, who played the most of three quarters at left guard, conducted himself very well. Don's work was never of the spectacular sort, but at his best he was a steady and thoroughly reliable lineman and very effective on defence. He was still slow in getting into plays, a fact which made him of less value than Joe Gafferty on attack. Even Harry Walton showed up better than Don when Brimfield had the ball. But neither Gafferty nor Walton was as strong on defence as Don.

Walton had been very earnestly striving all the week to capture the guard position, but the fact that Don had been played through most of the Morgan's game indicated that the latter was as yet a slight favourite in Coach Robey's estimation. During the week succeeding the Morgan's game the two rivals kept at it nip and tuck, and their team-mates looked on with interest. At practice Mr. Robey showed no favour to either, and each came in for his full share of criticism, but when, the next Saturday, the team journeyed away from home and played Cherry Valley, it was again Don who started the game between Thayer and Thursby and who remained in the line-up until the fourth period, by which time Brimfield had piled up the very satisfactory score of twenty-six points. In the final five minutes Cherry Valley managed to fool the visitors and get a forward pass off for a gain that placed the ball on Brimfield's fourteen yards, and from there her drop-kicker put the pigskin over the cross-bar and tallied three points. The game was uninteresting unless one was a partisan, and even then there were few thrills. Brimfield played considerably better than in the Morgan's game and emerged with no more important damages than a wrenched ankle, which fell to the share of Martin, who had taken Rollins's place in the last period.

Joe Gafferty came back to practice the following Monday, but was missing again a day or two later, and the school heard with some dismay that Joe's parents had written to Mr. Fernald and forbidden Joe to play any more football that year. Joe was inconsolable and went around for the next week or so looking like a lost soul. After that he accepted the situation and helped Mr. Boutelle coach the second. That second had by that time been shaken together into a very capable and smooth-running team, a team which was giving the first more and more trouble every day. Coach Robey had again levied on it for a player, taking Merton to the first when Gafferty was lost to him, and again Mr. Boutelle growled and protested and, finally, philosophically shrugged his shoulders. A week later Merton was released to the second once more and Pryme, who had been playing at right guard as a substitute for Tom Hall, was tried out on the other side of centre with good results. Pryme's advent as a contender for the left guard position complicated the battle between Don and Harry Walton, and until after the Southby game the trio of candidates indulged in a three-cornered struggle that was quite pretty to watch.

Unfortunately for Don, that struggle for supremacy threatened to affect his class standing, for it occupied so much of his thought that there was little left for study. When, however, the office dropped a hint and Mr. Daley presented an ultimatum, Don realised that he was taking football far too seriously, and, being a rather level-headed youth, he mended his ways. He expected, as a result, to find himself left behind in the race with Walton and Pryme, but, oddly enough, his game was in no degree affected so far as he could determine. In fact, within a few days the situation was simplified by the practical elimination of Pryme as a contender. This happened when, just before the Southby game, Tom Hall, together with eight other members of Mr. Moller's physics class went on probation, and Pryme was needed at right guard.

I have mentioned Tom's probation very casually, quite as if it was a matter of slight importance, but you may be sure that the school viewed it in no such way. Coming as it did little more than a fortnight before the big game, it was looked on as a dire catastrophe, no more and no less; and the school, which had laughed and chuckled over the incident which had caused the catastrophe, and applauded the participants in it, promptly turned their thumbs down when the effect became known and indignantly dubbed the affair "silly kid's play" and blamed Tom very heartily. How much of the blame he really deserved you shall judge for yourself, but the affair merits a chapter of its own.

CHAPTER XII
THE JOKE ON MR. MOLLER

AMY BYRD started it.

Or, perhaps, in the last analysis, Mr. Moller began it himself. Mr. Moller's first name was Caleb, a fact which the school was quick to seize on. At first he was just "Caleb," then "Caleb the Conqueror," and, finally, "The Conqueror." The "Conqueror" part of it was added in recognition of Mr. Moller's habit of attiring himself for the class room as for an afternoon tea. He was a new member of the faculty that fall and Brimfield required more than the few weeks which had elapsed since his advent to grow accustomed to his grandeur of apparel. Mr. Caleb Moller was a good-looking, in fact quite a handsome young man of twenty-five or six, well-built, tall and the proud possessor of a carefully trimmed moustache and Vandyke beard, the latter probably cultivated in the endeavour to add to his apparent age. He affected light grey trousers, fancy waistcoats of inoffensive shades, a frock coat, grey gaiters and patent leather shoes. His scarf was always pierced with a small black pearl pin. There's no denying that Mr. Moller knew how to dress or that the effect was pleasing. But Brimfield wasn't educated to such magnificence and Brimfield gasped loudly the first time Mr. Moller burst on its sight. Afterward it laughed until the novelty began to wear off. Mr. Moller was a capable instructor and a likeable man, although it took Brimfield all of the first term to discover the latter fact owing to the master's dignified aloofness. Being but a scant eight years the senior of some of his pupils, he perhaps felt it necessary to emphasise his dignity a little. By the last of October, however, the school had accepted Mr. Moller and was, possibly, secretly a little proud to have for a member of its faculty one who possessed such excellent taste in the matter of attire. He was universally voted "a swell dresser," and not a few of the older fellows set themselves to a modest emulation of his style. There remained, however, many unregenerate youths who continued to poke fun at "The Conqueror," and of these was Amy Byrd.

It isn't beyond the bounds of reason that jealousy may have had something to do with Amy's attitude, for Amy was "a swell dresser" himself and had a fine eye for effects of colour. Amy's combinations of lavender or dull rose or pearl-grey shirts, socks and ties were recognised masterpieces of sartorial achievement. The trouble with Amy was that when the tennis season was over he had nothing to interest himself in aside from maintaining a fairly satisfactory standing in class, and I'm sorry to say that Amy didn't find the latter undertaking wildly exciting. He was, therefore, an excellent subject for the mischief microbe, and the mischief microbe had long since discovered the fact. Usually Amy's escapades were harmless enough; for that matter, the present one was never intended to lead to any such unfortunate results as actually attended it; and in justice to Amy it should be distinctly stated that he would never have gone into the affair had he foreseen the end of it. But he couldn't see any further into the future than you or I, and so—yes, on the whole, I think it may be fairly said that Amy Byrd started it.

It was on a Tuesday, what time Amy should have been deep in study, that Clint Thayer, across the table, had his attention wrested from his book by the sound of deep, mirthful chuckles. He glanced over questioningly. Amy continued to chuckle until, being bidden to share the joke or shut up, he took Clint into his confidence. Clint was forced to chuckle some himself when he had heard Amy through, but the chuckles were followed by earnest efforts to dissuade his friend from his proposed scheme.

"He won't stand for it, Amy," Clint protested. "He will report the lot of you to Josh and you'll be in a peck of trouble. It would be terribly funny, all right, but you'd better not try it."

"Funny! My friend, it would be excruciating! And I certainly am going to have a stab at it. Let's see who will go into it. Steve

Edwards—no, Steve wouldn't, of course. Tom Hall will, I'll bet. And Roy Draper and Harry Wescott, probably. We ought to get as many of the fellows as we can. I wish you were in that class, Clint."

"I don't. You're a chump to try such a trick, Amy. You'll get pro for sure. Maybe worse. I don't believe Moller can take a joke; he's too haughty."

"Oh, rot! He will take it all right. Anyway, what kick can he have? We fellows have just as much right to——"

"You'll wish you hadn't," said Clint. "See if you don't!"

Clint's prophecy proved true, and Amy did wish he hadn't, but that was some days later, and just now he was far too absorbed in planning his little joke to trouble himself about what might happen as a result. As soon as study hour was over he departed precipitately from Number 14. Torrence and Clint saw no more of him until bedtime. Then his questions met only with more chuckles and evasion.

The result did not appear until two days later, which brings our tale to the forenoon of that unlucky Thursday preceeding the Southby contest. Mr. Moller's class in Physics 2 met at eleven o'clock that morning. Physics was an elective course with the Fifth Form and a popular one, many of the fellows taking it only to fill out their necessary eighteen hours a week. Mr. Moller, attired as usual with artistic nicety, sat in his swivel chair, facing the windows, and drummed softly on the top of the desk with immaculate finger-tips and waited for the class to assemble.

Had he been observing the arriving students instead of the tree-tops outside he might have noticed the peculiar fact that this morning, as though by common consent, the students were avoiding the first two rows of seats nearest the platform. But he didn't notice it. In fact, he didn't turn his head until the gong in the lower hall struck and, simultaneously, there sounded in the room the carefully-timed tread of many feet. Then "The Conqueror" swung around in his chair, felt for the black ribbon which held his tortoise shell glasses and, in the act of lifting the glasses to his well-shaped nose, paused and stared.

Down the side aisle of the room, keeping step, grave of mien, walked nine boys led by the sober-countenanced Amy Byrd. Each was attired in as near an approach to Mr. Moller's style as had been possible with the wardrobes at command. Not all—in fact, only two—wore frock coats, and not all had been able to supply themselves with light grey trousers, but the substitutions were very effective, and in no case was a fancy waistcoat wanting. Wing collars encircled every throat, grey silk scarves were tied with careful precision, stick-pins were at the proper careless tilt, spats, some grey, some tan, some black, covered each ankle, a handkerchief protruded a virgin corner from every right sleeve and over every vest dangled a black silk ribbon. That only a few of them ended in glasses was merely because the supply of those aids to vision had proved inadequate to the demand. Soberly and amidst an appalling silence the nine exquisites paced to the front of the room and disposed themselves in the first two rows.

Mr. Moller, his face extremely red, watched without word or motion. The rest of the class, their countenances too showing an unnatural ruddiness, likewise maintained silence and immobility until the last of the nine had shuffled his feet into place. Then there burst upon the stillness a snigger which, faint as it was, sounded startlingly loud. Whereupon pent up emotions broke loose and a burst of laughter went up that shook the windows.

It seemed for a minute that that laughter would never stop. Fellows rolled in their seats and beat futilely on the arms of their chairs, gasping for breath and sobriety. And through it all Mr. Moller stared in a sort of dazed amazement. And then, when the laughter had somewhat abated, he arose, one hand on the desk and the other agitatedly fingering his black ribbon, and the colour poured out of his cheeks, leaving them strangely pallid. And Amy, furtively studying him, knew that Clint had been right, that Mr. Moller couldn't take a joke, or, in any event, had no intention of taking this one. Amy wasn't frightened for himself, in fact he wasn't frightened at all, but he did experience a twinge of regret for the others whom he had led into the affair. Then Mr. Moller was speaking and Amy forgot regrets and listened.

"I am going to give you young gentlemen"—was it imagination on Amy's part or had the instructor placed the least bit of emphasis on the last word—"two minutes more in which to recover from your merriment. At the end of that time I shall expect you to be quiet and orderly and ready to begin this recitation." He drew his watch from his pocket and laid it on the desk. "So that you may enjoy this—this brilliant jest to the full, I'll ask the nine young gentleman in the front rows to stand up and face you. If you please, Hall, Stearns, Draper, Fanning, Byrd——"

It was several seconds before this request was responded to. Then Amy arose and, one by one, the others followed and faced the room. Amy managed to retain his expression of calm innocence, but the others were ill at ease and many faces looked very sheepish.

"Now, then," announced Mr. Moller quietly. "Begin, please. You have two minutes."

A dismal silence ensued, a silence broken at intervals by a nervous cough or the embarrassed shuffling of feet. Mr. Moller calmly divided his attention between the class and the watch. Surely never had one hundred and twenty seconds ticked themselves away so slowly. There was a noticeable disinclination on the part of the students to meet the gaze of the instructor, nor did they seem any more eager to view the various and generally painful emotions expressed on the countenances of the nine. At last Mr. Moller took up his watch and returned it with its dangling fob to his pocket, and as he did so some thirty sighs of relief sounded in the stillness.

"Time's up," announced the instructor. "Be seated, young gentlemen. Thank you very much." The nine sank gratefully into their chairs. "I am sure that we have all enjoyed your joke vastly. You must pardon me if, just at first, I seemed to miss the humour of it. I can assure you that I am now quite—quite sympathique. We are told that imitation is the sincerest flattery, and I accept the compliment in the spirit in which you have tendered it. Again I thank you."

Mr. Moller bowed gravely and sat down.

Glances, furtive and incredulous, passed from boy to boy. Amy heaved a sigh of relief. After all, then, Mr. Moller could take a joke! And for the first time since the inception of the brilliant idea Amy felt an emotion very much like regret! And then the recitation began.

That would have ended the episode had not Chance taken a hand in affairs. Mr. Fernald very seldom visited a class room during recitations. One could count such occurrences on one hand and the result would have sufficed for the school year. And yet today, for some reason never apparent to the boys, Mr. Fernald happened in.

Harry Westcott was holding forth when the principal's tread caught his attention. Westcott turned his head, saw and instantly stopped.

"Proceed, Westcott," said Mr. Fernald.

Westcott continued, stammeringly and much at random. Mr. Fernald quietly walked up the aisle to the platform. Mr. Moller arose and for a moment the two spoke in low tones. Then the principal nodded, smiled and turned to retrace his steps. As he did so his smiling regard fell upon the occupants of the two front rows. A look of puzzlement banished the smile. Bewilderment followed that. Westcott faltered and stopped altogether. A horrible silence ensued. Then Mr. Fernald turned an inquiring look upon the instructor.

"May I ask," he said coldly, "what this—this quaint exhibition is intended to convey?"

Mr. Moller hesitated an instant. Then: "I think I can explain it better, sir, later on," he replied.

Mr. Fernald bowed, again swept the offenders with a glance of withering contempt and took his departure. Mr. Moller looked troubledly after him before he turned to Westcott and said kindly: "Now, Westcott, we will go on, if you please."

What passed between principal and instructor later that day was not known, but the result of the interview appeared the next morning when Mr. Fernald announced in chapel that because they had seen fit to publicly insult a member of the faculty he considered it only just to publicly inform the following students that they were placed on probation until further notice. Then followed the names of Hall, Westcott, Byrd, Draper and five others. Mr. Fernald added that but for the intercession of the faculty member whom they had so vilely affronted the punishment would have been far heavier.

Nine very depressed youths took their departure from chapel that morning. To Tom Hall, since the edict meant that he could not play any more football that season, unless, which was scarcely probable, faculty relented within a week or so, the blow was far heavier than to any of the others. Being on probation was never a state to be sought for, but when one was in his last year at school and had looked forward to ending his football career in a blaze of glory, probation was just about as bad as being expelled. In fact, for a day or two Tom almost wished that Mr. Fernald had selected the latter punishment. What made things harder to bear was the attitude of coaches and players and the school at large. After the first shock of surprise and dismay, they had agreed with remarkable unanimity that Tom had not only played the fool, but had proved himself a traitor, and they didn't fail to let Tom know their verdict. For several days he was as nearly ostracised as it was possible to be, and those days were very unhappy ones for him.

Of course Tom was not utterly deserted. Steve Edwards stood by him firmly, fought public opinion, narrowly escaped a pitched battle with the president of the Sixth Form, worried Coach Robey to death with his demands that that gentler man intercede for Tom at the office and tried his best all the time to keep Tom's spirits up. Clint and Don and Tim and a few others remained steadfast, as did Amy, who, blaming himself bitterly for Tom's fix, had done everything he could do to atone. Following that edict in chapel, Amy had sought audience with Mr. Fernald and begged clemency for the others.

"You see, sir," Amy had pleaded earnestly, "I was the one who started it. The others would never have gone into it if I hadn't just simply made them. Why——"

Mr. Fernald smiled faintly. "You're trying to convince me, Byrd, that boys like Draper and Hall and Stearns and Westcott are so weak-willed that they allowed you to drag them into this thing against their better judgment and inclinations?"

"Yes, sir! At least—perhaps not exactly that, Mr. Fernald, but I—I nagged them and dared them, you see, sir, and they didn't like to be dared and they just did it to shut me up."

"It's decent of you, Byrd, to try to assume all the blame, but your story doesn't carry conviction. Even if it did, I should be sorely tempted to let the verdict stand, for I should consider boys who were so easily dragged into mischief badly in need of discipline. I do wish you'd tell me one thing, Byrd. How could a fellow, a manly, decent fellow like you, think up such a caddish trick? Wounding another man's feelings, Byrd, isn't really funny, if you stop to consider it."

"I didn't mean to hurt Mr. Moller's feelings, sir," replied Amy earnestly. "We—I thought it would just be a—a sort of a good joke to dress like him, sir, and—and get a laugh from the class. I'm sorry. I guess it was a pretty rotten thing to do, sir. Only I didn't think about it that way."

"I believe that. Since you've been here, Byrd, you've been into more or less mischief, but I've never known you to be guilty before of anything in such utterly bad taste. Unfortunately, however, I can't excuse you because you didn't think. You should have thought."

"Yes, sir," agreed Amy eagerly, "and I don't expect to be excused, sir. I only thought that maybe you'd let up on the others if you knew how it all happened. I thought maybe it would do just as well if you expelled me, sir, and let the other fellows off easy. Tom Hall——"

"I see. It's Hall who's worrying you, is it? You're afraid Hall's absence from the team may result disastrously! Possibly it will. If it does I shall be sorry, but Hall will have to take his medicine just like the rest of you. Perhaps this will teach you all to think a little before you act. No, Byrd, I shall have to refuse your offer. Expelling you would not be disciplining the rest, nor would it be an equitable division of punishment. The verdict must stand, my boy."

Amy went sorrowfully forth and announced the result to Clint. "I think he might have done what I wanted," he complained a trifle resentfully.

"You're an utter ass," said Clint with unflattering conviction. "What good would it do you to get fired in your last year?"

"None, but if he'd have let the others off——"

"Do you suppose that the others would have agreed to any such bargain? They're not kids, even if you try to make them out so. They went into the thing with their eyes open and are just as much to blame as you are. They wouldn't let you be the goat, you idiot!"

"They needn't have known anything about it, Clint. Oh, well, I suppose there's no use fussing. I don't care about the others. It's Tom I'm sorry for. And the team, too. Pryme can't fill Tom's shoes, and we'll get everlastingly walloped, and it'll be my fault, and——"

"Piffle! Tom's a good player, one of the best, but he isn't the whole team. Pryme will play the position nearly as well. I'm sorry for Tom, too, but he's the one who will have to do the worrying, I guess. Now you buck up and quit looking like a kicked cur."

"If only the fellows didn't have it in for him the way they have," mourned Amy. "Everyone's down on him and he knows it and he's worried to death about it. They're a lot of rotters! After the way Tom's worked on that team ever since he got on it! Why, he's done enough for the school if he never played another lick at anything! And I'll tell you another thing. Someone's going to get licked if I hear any more of this knocking!"

"You'll have to lick most of the school then," replied Clint calmly. "Try not to be a bigger chump than nature made you, Amy. You can't blame the fellows for being a bit sore at Tom. I am myself. Only I realise that he didn't mean to get into trouble with the office, and the rest of them don't, I reckon. It'll all blow over in a few days. Cheer up. A month from now you won't care a whoop."

"If we're beaten by Claflin I'll get out of school," answered Amy dolefully.

"All right, son, but don't begin to pack your trunk yet. We won't be."

CHAPTER XIII
SOUTHBY YIELDS

THE game with Southby Academy that week was played away from home. As a general thing Southby was not a formidable opponent and last year's contest had resulted in a 17 to 3 win for Brimfield. But this Fall Southby had been piling up larger scores

71

against her opponents and her stock had risen. Consequently Brimfield, being deprived of Tom Hall's services at right guard and of Rollins's at full-back, journeyed off that morning more than a little doubtful of the result of the coming conflict. Most of the school went along, since Southby was easily reached by trolley and at a small outlay for fares, and Brimfield was pretty well deserted by one o'clock. Out of some one hundred and eighty students a scant forty remained behind, and of that two-score we can guess who nine were!

The game started with Edwards at left end for Brimfield, Thayer at left tackle, Gilbert at left guard, Peters at centre, Pryme at right guard, Sturges at right tackle, Holt at right end, Carmine at quarter, St. Clair at left half, Otis at right half and Martin at full-back. Later on, toward the end of the second quarter, Thursby went in at centre, and in the fourth period several substitutes had their chances, amongst them Harry Walton.

Walton had begun to realise that he was playing a losing game. Since Pryme had been shifted back to the right side of the line Don Gilbert had come more than ever to the fore and Harry had spent a deal more time with the substitute squad in practice and on the bench during scrimmage than he approved of. Harry had a very special reason for wanting to win that left guard position and to play in it during the Claflin game, and this afternoon, sitting on the side line with a dozen other blanketed substitutes and enviously watching Don in the coveted place, his brain evolved a plan that promised so well that by the time the second period had started he was looking almost cheerful. And that is saying a good deal, since Harry Walton's countenance very seldom expressed cheer.

Southby showed her mettle within five minutes of the kick-off, when, getting the ball on a fumble on her forty-five yard line, she tore off thirty-three yards on a complicated double-pass play and then, ripped another down from the astonished adversary. On the Maroon-and-Grey's nine yards, however, her advance was halted, and after two downs had resulted in a loss, she sent her kicker back and placed a neat drop over the cross-bars, scoring three points before the stop-watch had ticked off six minutes of playing time.

That score was apparently just what Brimfield needed to bring her to her senses, for the rest of the period was marked by brilliant defensive work on her part, followed toward the end of the twelve minutes by some equally good attacks. When the teams changed places Brimfield had the pigskin on Southby's thirty-eight yards with four to go on third down. A forward pass, Carmine to St. Clair, produced three of the required four and Martin slipped through between left guard and tackle for the rest. After that ten well-selected plays took the ball to the sixteen yards. But there Southby rallied, and Steve Edwards, dropping back as if to kick, tore off five more around the left end. A touchdown seemed imminent now, and the hundred or so Brimfield rooters shouted and cheered madly enough. But two plunges at the right of the Southby line were stopped for scant gain and, with Martin back, a forward pass to Holt missed that youth and fell plump into the hands of a Southby end, and it was Southby's ball on her eight yards when the dust of battle had cleared away.

That was Brimfield's last chance to score in that half and when the whistle sounded Southby had the pigskin once more in her adversary's territory.

So far the teams had proved evenly matched in all departments, with a possible slight superiority in punting belonging to the visitors. St. Clair and Martin divided the punting between them and together they managed to outmatch the efforts of the Southby kicker. In the line both teams were excellent on defence, and both showed similar weakness in attack. In Tom Hall's place Pryme had worked hard and had, on the whole, done all that was expected of him. But he wasn't Tom Hall, and no amount of coaching would make him Tom's equal that Fall. Pryme lacked two factors: weight and, more especially, experience. Southby had made some good gains through him in the first half and would have made more had not Peters and Sturges helped him valiantly. As to the backfields, a disinterested spectator would have liked the Brimfield players a bit the better, less perhaps for what they actually accomplished that day than for what they promised. Even with Rollins out, the Maroon-and-Grey backs showed a fine and consistent solidarity that was lacking in the opponents. Coach Robey was a believer in team-play as opposed to the exploitation of stars, while Southby, with a remarkable half-back in the person of a blonde-haired youth named Elliston, had built her backfield about one man. As a consequence, when Elliston was smothered, as was frequently the case, since Southby's opponents naturally played for him all the time, the play was stopped. Today Captain Edwards had displayed an almost uncanny ability to "get" Elliston when the play was in his direction, and so far the blonde-haired star had failed to distinguish himself save in that one thirty-three-yard gambol at the beginning of the contest. What might happen later was problematical, but so far Brimfield had solved Elliston fairly well.

A guard seldom has an opportunity to pose in the limelight, and so you are not to hear that Don pulled off any brilliant feats that

73

afternoon. What he did do was to very thoroughly vindicate Mr. Robey's selection of him for Gafferty's position by giving an excellent impersonation of a concrete block on defence and by doing rather better than he had ever done before when his side had the ball. Don had actually speeded up considerably, much as Tim had assured him he could, and while he was still by no means the snappiest man in the line, nor was ever likely to be, he was seldom far behind his fellows. For that matter the whole line of forwards was still much slower than Mr. Robey wanted them at that time of year, and Don showed up not badly in comparison. After all, what is needed in a guard is, first and foremost, fighting spirit, and Don had that. If he was a bit slower to sense a play, a little later in getting into it, at least when he did start he started hard and tackled hard and always played it safe. In the old days when a guard had only his small territory between centre and tackle to cover, Don would have been an ideal player for the position, but now, when a guard's duties are to free-lance, so to speak, from one end of the line to the other and to get into the play no matter where it comes, Don's qualifications were more limited. A guard in these amazing times is "soldier and sailor too," and Don, who liked to deal with one idea at a time, found it a bit confusing to have to grapple with a half-dozen!

Brimfield returned to the battle at the beginning of the second half highly resolved to take no more fooling from her opponent. Fortune ordered it that the south goal should fall to her portion and that a faint but dependable breeze should spring up between the halves. That breeze changed Coach Robey's plans, and the team went on with instructions to kick its way to within scoring distance and then batter through the line at any cost. And so the spectators were treated to a very pretty punting exhibition by both teams, for, wisely or unwisely, Southby accepted the challenge and punted almost as often as her adversary. That third period supplied many thrills but no scoring, for although Brimfield did manage to get the ball on Southby's twenty-five-yard line when a back fumbled, the advantage ended there. Two rushes failed, a forward pass grounded and when St. Clair tried to skirt his own left end he was pulled down just short of his distance and Southby soon punted out of danger.

When time was called both teams made several substitutions. Don yielded his place to Harry Walton, Crewe went in at right tackle and McPhee took Carmine's position at quarter. With the advantage of the wind no longer hers, Brimfield abandoned the kicking game and used her backfield for all it was worth. From the middle of the field to Southby's thirty yards she went without much difficulty, St. Clair, Martin and Tim Otis carrying the ball for short but consistent gains. But at the thirty Southby braced and captured the pigskin on downs by a matter of inches. It was then that Elliston repeated. Following two attempts at Pryme's position, which yielded a scant four yards, Elliston got away around Steve Edwards's end and, with some good interference for the first ten or twelve yards, passed the whole field except McPhee and was only brought down by that player after he had run to Brimfield's twenty-six yards.

Southby's adherents cheered wildly and demanded a touchdown, and it looked for awhile as though their team was to give them what they asked for. Southby twice poked a back through the centre of the maroon-and-grey line and then tore off ten yards around Clint Thayer, Steve Edwards being put wholly out of the play. Then, however, Brimfield dug her cleats and held the enemy, giving a very heartening exhibition of stubborn defence, and again Southby decided that half a loaf was better than none and tried a field-goal. She ought never to have got it, for the left side of her line was torn to ribbons by the desperate defenders. But she did, nevertheless, the ball in some miraculous manner slipping through the upstretched hands and leaping bodies and just topping the bar.

Those three added points seemed to spell defeat for Brimfield, and many of her supporters in the stand conceded the victory to Southby then and there. But the team refused to view the matter in that light and came back fighting hard. With only some seven minutes of the twelve left, McPhee opened the line when Southby had finally been forced to punt from her twelve yards and St. Clair had caught on his forty-five, and started a series of direct-pass plays that, coming as they did on the heels of an afternoon of close-formation plays, confused the enemy until the ball had been planted ncar her thirty-five yards. Brimfield fought desperately then, closing her line again and sending Edwards off on an end-around run that took the pigskin eight yards nearer the last white mark.

It was then that St. Clair really showed what was in him. Four times he took the ball and four times he plunged, squirming, fighting, through the Southby centre and, with the Brimfield shouts cheering him on, put the leather down at last on Southby's eighteen. Otis got three off left tackle and McPhee tried the same end for no gain. Martin went back and, faking a kick, threw forward to Edwards, who romped to the nine yards before he was smothered. It was fourth down then, with less than a yard to go, and St. Clair was called on. A delayed-pass did the business and Southby was digging her toes into her seven yards. Martin slid off right tackle for two, bringing the ball nearly in front of goal, and the defenders again fell back.

Carmine was sent in again for McPhee and Lawton took Pryme's place. Carmine evidently brought instructions, for Captain Edwards fell back to kicking position after the conference, and the ball was passed to him. But with only five to go and three downs to do it in a drop-kick was not likely, especially as three points would still leave Brimfield beaten, and so Southby disregarded the bluff. But if a kick was out of the question a forward pass was not, and it was a forward pass that Southby set herself for. And so, with her ends drawn out and her backs spread, the touchdown came easily. For Steve faked a throw to the right, where Holt apparently waited, and then dashed straight ahead, the ball against his ribs, his head down and his feet flying, struck the hastily-formed massing of Southby's centre like a battering ram and literally tore his way through until, when he was at last pulled down, he was five yards over the line!

Since Brimfield needed that goal badly, Rollins, in spite of bandages, was sent in for Martin, and, when Carmine had canted the ball to his liking, very calmly put it squarely between the uprights above the bar.

The remaining minute and a half of play brought no results and Brimfield trotted off victor by the narrow margin of one point, while her adherents flowed across the field cheering and flaunting their banners in triumph.

CHAPTER XIV
WALTON WRITES A NOTE

THE Southby game was played on the sixth of November, a fortnight before the final contest with Claflin School, and practically marked the end of the preparatory season. Brimfield would meet her blue-legged rival with what plays she had already learned and the time for instruction was passed. The remaining two weeks, which held but ten playing days, would be devoted to perfecting plays already known, to polishing off the rough angles of attack and defence and to learning a new set of signals as a matter of precaution. Those ten days were expected to work a big improvement in the team. Whether they would or not remained to be seen.

On the whole, Brimfield had passed through a successful

season. She had played seven games, of which she had lost one, won five and tied one. Next week's adversary, Chambers, would in all likelihood supply a sixth victory, in which case the Maroon-and-Grey would face Claflin with a nearly clean slate. Claflin, on her part, had hung up a rather peculiar record that Fall. She had played one more game than Brimfield, had won four, lost one and tied three. She had started out strongly, had had a slump in mid-season and was now, from all evidence at hand, recovering finely. On comparative scores there was little to choose between the rivals. If any perceptible advantage belonged to Brimfield it was only because she had maintained a steadier pace.

There was a lay-off for most of the first-string players on Monday, a fact which gave Harry Walton a chance to conduct himself very capably at left guard during the four ten-minute periods of scrimmage with the second. Don didn't go near the field that afternoon and so was saved any of the uneasiness which the sight of Walton's performance might have caused him. Rollins got back for a short workout and showed few signs of his injury. The second team, profiting by some scouting done by Coach Boutelle and Joe Gafferty on Saturday, tried out the Claflin formation and such Claflin plays as had been fathomed against the first team and made some good gains thereby until the second-string players solved them. On Tuesday Harry Walton disgruntledly found himself again relegated to the bench during most of the practice game and saw Don open holes in the second team's line in a style that more than once brought commendation from Coach Robey. Walton glowered from the bench until Cotter disgustedly asked if he felt sick. Whereupon Walton grinned and Cotter, with a sigh, begged him to scowl again!

The first team presented its full strength that afternoon, and Mr. Boutelle's Claflin plays made little headway. With Rollins back in place, the first team scored almost at will during three periods, and even after an entirely new backfield was put in it continued to smash the second up very effectually. Mr. Boutelle scolded and raved and threatened, but all to scant purpose. The first got its plays off very smoothly, played low and hard and, for once, played together. The final score that day was the biggest ever piled up in a practice contest, 30 to 3. Had Mr. Robey allowed Rollins to try goals from touchdowns it would have been several points larger.

Tom Hall had so far carefully avoided the field, but today he appeared there and sat in the stand with Roy Draper and tried his best to be cheerful. But his best wasn't very good. Already the feeling against him had largely subsided, and the school, realising, perhaps, that Tom's loss to the team did not necessarily spell defeat for it, was inclined to be sorry for him. But Tom didn't realise that, since he still kept to himself and was suspicious of advances. He hadn't quarrelled with the school's verdict, but it had hurt him and, as he didn't like being hurt any more than most of us, he avoided the chance of it. In those days he stuck pretty close to his room, partly because the office required it and partly because he had no heart for mingling with his fellows. Roy Draper had to plead long and earnestly that afternoon to get him to the gridiron. As badly as he felt about losing his place on the team, however, Tom didn't begrudge Pryme his good fortune, and he was honestly pleased to see that the latter, in spite of his deficiencies, would doubtless fill the right guard position very capably in the Claflin game. He studied Pryme's work attentively that afternoon, criticised it and praised it and showed no trace of animosity.

"He will do all right," he confided to Roy. "Crewe will help him a lot, and so will Thursby. If he could use his hands a bit better he'd be fine. He holds himself nicely, doesn't he? On his toes all the time. I hate to see a lineman play flat-footed. That's one trouble with Don Gilbert. Don's doing a heap better than he did last year, though. I guess he's every bit as good as Joe Gafferty. He's a regular whale on defence, isn't he? He's a queer chap, Don, but a mighty nice one."

"Don," replied Roy in his somewhat didactic manner, "is the sort of fellow I'd pick out to be cast away on a desert island with. He isn't so scintillant, you know, but he'd wear forever."

"That's him to a T." Tom chuckled. "They tell me Harry Walton is as mad as a hatter because Don butted in and grabbed that position away from him. Can't say I altogether blame him, either. That is, there's no use getting mad about it, but it is tough luck. Harry isn't a half-bad guard, either."

"If he can play good football," answered Roy, "I'm glad to know it. I've always wondered what Walton was for."

Tom laughed. "Oh, he isn't so bad, I guess. His manner's against him."

"I've noticed it," said Roy drily. "Also his looks and his remarks and a number of other things. Larry Jones says he comes from the best sort of family."

"A fellow's family doesn't prove anything, I guess."

"Evidently not. There's the whistle. Let's go back." Presently Roy added, as they headed for Torrence: "I can quite understand why Walton's family sent him to school."

"Why they sent him to school?" repeated Tom questioningly.

"Yes, it was to get rid of him."

"You've certainly got your little hammer with you," said Tom, with a smile. "What's Harry done to you?"

"Not a thing. I wouldn't advise him to, either. I just don't like him, Tom. Can't stand being in the same room with him. Well, see you later, old chap. And, say, think over what I said about—you know."

"Oh, that's all right," replied Tom, with a shrug of his broad shoulders. "Fellows can think what they like about me. I don't blame them. But you can't expect me to like it!"

"I know, Tom, but they don't feel that way now. It was just for a day or two. I've heard a lot of fellows say lately that it's nonsense blaming you, Tom. So come out of your shell, like a sensible chap, and show that you don't feel any—any ill-will."

"Well, I don't, I suppose. As for coming out of my shell, I'll be crawling out pretty soon. Don't bother about me, Roy. I'm feeling fine. So long."

Perhaps what Tom really meant was that he was feeling a whole lot better than he had a few days before, for he certainly had not become quite reconciled to the loss of his position with the team. He was getting used to the idea, but he wasn't happy over it. When he squarely faced the fact that when Claflin came trotting onto the field on the twentieth he would be sitting in the grand stand instead of being out there in togs, his heart sank miserably and he hardly knew whether he wanted to kick something or get off in a corner and cry. At such moments the question of whether his school fellows liked him or detested him bothered little. If he could only play against Claflin, he assured himself, the school might hate him to its heart's content!

Going on to Billings and his room, he considered what Roy had told him of the altered sentiment toward him, but somehow he didn't seem to care so much today. Watching practice had brought back the smart, and being liked or disliked seemed a little thing beside the bigger trouble. Still, he thought, if Roy was right perhaps he had better meet fellows half-way. There was no use in being a grouch. As a starter and in order to test the accuracy of Roy's statement, he decided that he would drop in on Carl Bennett, who roomed in Number 3. Bennett was a chap he rather respected and, while they had never been very close friends, Tom had seen a good deal of the other during the Fall. But Bennett was not in and Tom was making his way back to the stairs when the door of Number 6 opened and Harry Walton came out. Perhaps it was Roy's dressing-down of that youth that prompted Tom to be more decent to him than usual. At all events, Tom stopped and hailed him and they conversed together on their way up the stairs. It wasn't until later that Tom, recalling Harry's grudge against Don, wondered what had taken him to the latter's room. Then he concluded that Harry had probably been calling on Tim, and thought no more of it. Just now he asked Harry how he was getting on with the team and was a little puzzled when Harry replied: "All right, I guess. Of course, Gilbert's got the call right now, but I'm going to beat him out before the big game. Did you see practice today?"

"Yes. You fellows put up a great game, Harry."

"I didn't get into it for more than ten minutes. Robey's playing Don Gilbert for all he knows." Harry laughed disagreeably. "Robey's a bit of a fox."

"How's that!" Tom inquired.

"Oh, he's sort of keeping me guessing, you see. Thinks I'll get worried and dig harder."

"Huh. I see. You seem mighty certain of that place, Harry."

"Sure, I'm certain. You just wait and see, old top." Harry nodded and entered his room across the hall, leaving Tom a trifle more sympathetic toward Roy's estimation of him. Walton certainly did have a disagreeable manner, he reflected.

As a matter of fact, Harry hadn't been calling on anyone in Number 6 for the simple reason that he had found no one at home. Moreover, he had expected to find no one, for he had left Tim at the gymnasium and seen Don and Harry Westcott sitting in the window of the latter's room in Torrence as he passed. What he had done was leave a hastily scrawled note for Don on the table in there, a note which Don discovered an hour later and which at once puzzled and disturbed him.

"Come up and see me after supper will you," the note read, with a superb disdain of punctuation, "I want to see you. Important. H. Walton."

"What's he want to see you about?" asked Tim when Don tossed the note to him to read.

"I don't know." Don frowned thoughtfully.

"I hope he isn't going to make trouble about that old business."

"What old business?" asked Tim carelessly, more interested in a set of bruised knuckles than anything else just then.

"Why, you know Harry saw us climbing in the window that night."

"Saw us climb—Well, what of it? That was years ago. Why should he want to make trouble about that? And how could he do it? I'd like to see him start anything with me."

80

"Oh, well, I just happened to think of that."

"More likely he's going to ask you to break a leg or something so he can get your place," chuckled Tim. "Don't you do it, Don, if he does. It doesn't pay to be too obliging. Ready for eats?"

"In a minute." Don dropped the note and began his toilet, but he didn't speak again until they were on their way down the stairs. Then: "If it should be that," he remarked, "I wouldn't know whether to punch his head or laugh at him."

"Don't take any chances," advised Tim grimly. "Punch his head. Better still, bring the glad tidings to me and let me do it. Why, if that idiot threatened to open his face about us I'd give him such a walloping that his own folks wouldn't recognise the remnants! Gee, but I'm hungry tonight! Toddle along faster and let's get there before Rollins and Holt and the rest swipe all the grub."

CHAPTER XV
A PROPOSITION

DON sought Harry Walton's room soon after supper was over and found neither Harry nor his room-mate, Jim Rose, at home. He lighted the droplight, found a magazine several months old and sat down to wait. He had, however, scarcely got into a story before Harry appeared.

"Hello," greeted the latter. "Sorry I was late. Had to stop at the library for a book." In proof of it he tossed a volume to the table. "I asked you to come up here, Gilbert, because I have a proposition to make and I thought you wouldn't want anyone around." Harry seated himself, took one knee into his clasped hands and smiled at the visitor. It was a peculiarly unattractive smile, Don decided.

"Proposition?" Don frowned perplexedly. "What sort of a proposition, Walton?"

"Well, I'll tell you. It's like this, Gilbert. You see, old man, you and I are fighting like the mischief for the left guard position and so far it's about nip-and-tuck, isn't it?"

Don viewed the speaker with some surprise. "Is it?" he asked. "I thought I had rather the best of it, Walton."

Harry smiled and shrugged. "That's only Robey's foxiness. I'm not saying he might not pick you for the place in the end, of course, but I stand just as good a show. Robey doesn't like to show his hand.

81

He likes to keep you guessing. I'm willing to bet that if nothing happened he'd drop you next week and stick me in there. Of course you might get in for awhile in the Claflin game, if I got hurt, but I wouldn't advise you to bank much on that because I'm rather lucky about not getting hurt. Honestly, Gilbert, I don't really think you've got much of a chance of final selection."

Don observed his host's countenance with some bewilderment. "Well," he said at last, "that may be so or not. What is it you want me to do?"

"I'll tell you." Harry tried hard to look ingenuous, but only succeeded in grinning like a catfish. "It's this way. My folks are coming up for the Claflin game; father and mother and kid brother, you know. Well, naturally, I'd like to have them see me play. They think I'm going to, of course, because I've mentioned it once or twice in my letters. I'd feel pretty cheap if they came up here and watched me sitting on the bench all through the game. See what I mean, old man?"

Don nodded and waited.

"Well, so I thought that as your chance is pretty slim anyway maybe you wouldn't mind dropping out. I wouldn't ask you to if I really thought you had much chance, you know, Gilbert."

"Oh! That's it? Well, I'm sorry if you're folks are going to be disappointed, Walton, but I don't feel quite like playing the goat on that account. You might just write them and sort of prepare them for the shock, mightn't you? Tell them there's a bare chance that you won't get into the fracas, you know. I would. It would soften the blow for them, Walton."

Walton scowled. "Don't be funny," he said shortly. "I've given you the chance to drop out gracefully, Gilbert, and you're a fool not to take it."

"But why should I drop out! Don't you suppose I want to play in the Claflin game just as much as you do?"

"Perhaps you do, but you won't play in it any way you figure it. If you don't quit willingly you'll quit the other way. I'm giving you a fair chance, that's all. You've only got to make believe you're sick or play sort of rottenly a couple of times. That will do the trick for you and there won't be any other trouble."

"Say, what are you hinting at?" demanded Don quietly. "What have you got up your sleeve?"

"Plenty, Gilbert. I've got enough up my sleeve to get you fired from school."

There was a moment of silence. Then Don nodded thoughtfully. "So that's it, is it?" he murmured.

82

"That's it, old man." Harry grinned. "Think it over now."

"What do you think you've got on me?" asked Don.

"I don't think. I know that you and three other fellows helped put out that fire that night and that you didn't get back to hall until long after ten-thirty." Harry dropped his knee, thrust his hands into his pockets, leaned back in his chair and viewed Don triumphantly. "I don't want to go to faculty with it, Gilbert, although it's really my duty and I certainly shall if you force me."

"Hm," mused Don. "But wouldn't faculty wonder why you'd been so long about it?"

"Probably. I'd have to tell the truth and——"

"I guess that would hurt," interpolated the other drily.

"And explain that I'd tried to shield you fellows, but that my conscience had finally prevailed." And Harry grinned broadly. "Josh wouldn't like it, but he wouldn't do anything to me. What he'd do to you, though, would be a plenty, Gilbert. It would be expulsion, and you know that as well as I do."

"Yes, I do." Don dropped his gaze to his hands and was silent a moment. Then: "Of course you've thought of what it would mean to you, Walton? I wouldn't be likely to keep you out of it, you know."

Harry shrugged. "Fellows might talk some, but I'd only be doing my duty. As long as my conscience was clear——"

"You're a dirty pup, Walton," said Don, "and if I wasn't afraid of getting the mange I'd give you the beating you deserve."

"Calling names won't get you anything, Gilbert. I'm not afraid of anything you could do to me, anyway. I may be a pup, but I'm where I can make you sit up and beg, and I'm going to do it."

"You think you are," said Don contemptuously. "Let me tell you now that I'd rather be fired a dozen times than make any bargains with a common skunk like you!"

"That means you want me to go ahead and tell Josh, does it?"

"It means that you can do anything you want to, Walton." Don stood up. "But if you do go to faculty with the story you'll get the worst licking you ever had or heard of, and fellows will make it so unpleasant here for you that you won't stay much longer than I do. Now you think it over!"

"What fellows say or think won't hurt me a mite, thank you, and I'm not afraid of you or any of your friends, Gilbert. Wait a minute now. We're not through yet."

"I am, thanks," replied Don, moving toward the door.

"Oh, no you're not. You may feel heroic and all that and too mad to give in just now, but you're not considering what it will mean if you make me squeal to faculty. Why, we wouldn't have a ghost of a show with Claflin!"

"I thought you considered yourself quite as good a guard as me, Walton," answered Don.

"I do, old man. But I don't think I'm able to take the places of all the other fellows who would be missing from the team."

Don turned, with his hand on the door-knob, and stared startledly. "What do you mean by that?" he asked.

"I thought that would fetch you," chuckled Harry. "I mean that you're not the only one who would quit the dear old school, Gilbert. You haven't forgotten, I suppose, that there were three other fellows mixed up in the business?"

"No, but faculty would have to know more than I'd tell them before they'd find out who the others were."

"Oh, you wouldn't have to tell them, old man."

"Meaning you would? You don't know, Walton."

"Don't I, though? You bet I do! I know every last one of them!"

"You told me——"

"Oh, I let you think I didn't, Gilbert. No use telling everything you know."

"I don't believe it!" But, in spite of the statement, Don did believe it and was trying to realise what it meant. .

"Don't be a fool! Why wouldn't I know? If I could see you why couldn't I see Clint Thayer and Tim Otis and Tom Hall? You were all as plain as daylight. Of course, Tom's out of it, anyway, but I guess losing a left tackle and a right half-back a week before the game would put rather a dent in our chances, what? And that's just what will happen if you make me go to Josh with the story!"

"You wouldn't!" challenged Don, but there was scant conviction in his tone. Harry shrugged his shoulders.

"Oh, I'd rather not. I don't want to play on a losing team, and that's what I'd be doing, but you see I've sort of set my heart on playing right guard a week from Saturday, Gilbert, and I hate to be disappointed. Hate to disappoint my folks, too."

"They must be proud of you!"

"They are, take it from me." Harry's smile vanished and he looked ugly as he went on. "Don't be a fool, Gilbert! You'd do the same thing yourself if you had the chance. You're playing the hypocrite, and you know it. I've got you dead to rights and I mean to make the most of it. If you don't get off the team inside of two days I'll go to Josh and tell him everything I know. It isn't pretty, maybe, but it's playing your hand for what there is in it, and that's my way! Now you sit down again and just think it all over, Gilbert. Take all the time you want. And remember this, too. If I keep my mouth shut you've got to keep yours shut. No blabbing to Tim Otis or Clint Thayer or anyone else. This is just between you and me, old man. Now what do you say?"

"The thing's as crazy as it is rotten, Walton! How am I to get off the team without having it look funny?"

"And how much do I care whether it looks funny or not? That's up to you. You can play sick or you can get out there and mix your signals a few times or you can bite Robey in the leg. I don't give a hang what you do so long as you do it, and do it between now and Saturday. That's right, sit down and look at it sensibly. Mull it over awhile. There's no hurry."

CHAPTER XVI
DON VISITS THE DOCTOR

"WHAT did Walton want of you?" asked Tim a half-hour later, when the occupants of Number 6 were settled at opposite sides of the table for study.

"Walton?" repeated Don vaguely. "Oh, nothing especial."

"Nothing especial? Then why the mysterious summons? Did he make any crack about that little escapade of ours?"

"He mentioned it. Shut up and let me get to work, Tim."

"Mentioned it how? What did he say? Any chance of beating him up? I've always had a longing, away down deep inside me, Donald, to place my fist violently against some portion of Walton's—er—facial contour. Say, that's good, isn't it? Facial contour's decidedly good, Don."

"Fine," responded the other listlessly.

Tim peered across at him under the droplight. "Say, you look as if you'd lost a dozen dear friends. Anything wrong? Look here, has Walton been acting nasty?"

"Don't be a chump, Tim. I'm all right. Or, anyway, I'm only sort of—sort of tired. Dry up and let me stuff."

"Oh, very well, but you needn't be so haughty about it. I don't want to share your secrets with dear Harry. Everyone to his taste, as the old lady said when she kissed the cow."

Tim's sarcasm, however, brought no response, and presently, after growling a little while he pawed his books over and dropped the subject, to Don's relief, and silence fell. Don made a fine pretence of studying, but most of the time he couldn't have told what book lay before him. When the hour was up Tim, who had by then returned to his usual condition of cheerful good nature, tried to induce Don to go over to Hensey to call on Larry Jones, who, it seemed, had perfected a most novel and marvellous trick with a ruler and two glasses of water. But Don refused to be enticed and Tim went off alone, gravely cautioning his room-mate against melancholia.

"Try to keep your mind off your troubles, Donald. Think of bright and happy things, like me or the pretty birds. Remember that nothing is ever quite as bad as we think it is, that every line has a silver clouding and that—that it's always dawnest before the dark. Farewell, you old grouch!"

Don didn't have to pretend very hard the next day that he was feeling ill, for an almost sleepless night, spent in trying to find some way out of his difficulties, had left him hollow-eyed and pale. Breakfast had been a farce and dinner a mere empty pretence, and between the two meals he had fared illy in classes. It was scarcely more than an exaggeration to tell Coach Robey that he didn't feel well enough to play, and the coach readily believed him and gave him over to the mercies of Danny Moore.

The trainer tried hard to get Don to enumerate some tangible symptoms, but Don could only repeat that he was dreadfully tired and out of sorts. "Eat anything that didn't agree with you?" asked Danny.

"No, I didn't eat much of anything. I didn't have any appetite."

"Sure, that was sensible, anyway. I'll be after giving you a tonic, me boy. Take it like I tell you, do ye mind, keep off your feet and get a good sleep. After breakfast come to me in the gym and I'll have a look at you."

Don took the tonic—when he thought of it—ate a fair supper and went early to bed, not so much in the hope of curing his ailment as because he couldn't keep his eyes open any longer. He slept pretty well, but was dimly conscious of waking frequently during the night, and when morning came felt fully as tired as when he had retired. Breakfast was beyond him, although Mr. Robey, his attention drawn to Don by Harry Walton's innocent "You're looking pretty bum, Gilbert," counselled soft boiled eggs and hot milk. Don dallied with the eggs and drank part of the milk and was glad to escape as soon as he could.

Danny gave him a very thorough inspection in the rubbing room after breakfast, but could find nothing wrong. "Sure, you're as sound as Colin Meagher's fiddle, me boy. Where is it it hurts ye?"

"It doesn't hurt anywhere, Danny," responded Don. "I'm all right, I suppose, only I don't feel—don't feel very fit."

"A bit fine, you are, and I'm thinking you'd better lay off the work for today. Be outdoors as much as you can, but don't be tiring yourself out. Have you taken the tonic like I told ye?"

"I've taken enough of the beastly stuff," answered Don listlessly.

Danny laughed. "Sure, it's the fine-tasting medicine, lad. Keep at it. And listen to me, now. If you want to play agin Claflin, Donny, you do as I'm tellin' you and don't be thinkin' you know more about it than I do. Sure, Robey won't look at ye at all, come a week from tomorrow, if you don't brace up."

"Oh, I'm all right, Danny, thanks. Maybe if I rest off today I'll be fine tomorrow."

"That's what I'm tellin' you. See that ye do it."

That afternoon he watched practice from the bench without getting into togs and saw Harry Walton play at left guard. He would much rather have remained away from the field, but to have done so might, he thought, have looked queer. Coach Robey was solicitous about him, but apparently did not take his indisposition very seriously. "'Take it easy, Gilbert," he said, "and don't worry. You'll be all right for tomorrow, I guess. You've been working pretty hard, my boy. Better pull a blanket over your shoulders. This breeze is rather biting. Can't have you laid up for long, you know."

Harry Walton performed well that afternoon, playing with a vim and dash that was something of a revelation to his team-mates. Tim was evidently troubled when he walked back to hall with Don after practice. "For the love of mud, Don," he pleaded, "get over it and come back! Did you see the way Walton played today? If he gets in tomorrow and plays like that against Chambers Robey'll be handing him the place! What the dickens is wrong with you, anyway?"

"I'm just tired," responded Don.

"Tired!" Tim was puzzled. "What for? You haven't worked since day before yesterday. What you've got is malaria or something. Tell you what we'll do, Don; we'll beat it over to the doctor's after supper, eh?"

But Don shook his head. "Danny's tonic is all I need," he said. "I dare say I'll be feeling great in the morning."

"You dare say you will! Don't you feel sure you will? Because I've got to tell you, Donald, that this is a plaguy bad time to get laid off, son. If you're not a regular little Bright Eyes by Monday Robey'll can you as sure as shooting!"

"I wouldn't much care if he did," muttered Don.

"You wouldn't much—— Say, are you crazy?" Tim stopped short on the walk and viewed his chum in amazement. "Is it your brain that's gone back on you? Don't you want to play against Claflin?"

"I suppose so. Yes, of course I do, but——"

"Then don't talk like a piece of cheese! You'll come with me to the doctor after supper if I have to drag you there by one heel!"

And so go he did, and the doctor looked at his tongue and felt his pulse and "pawed him over," as Don put it, and ended by patting him on the back and accepting a nice bright half-dollar—half-price to Academy students—in exchange for a prescription.

"You're a little nervous," said the doctor. "Thinking too much about that football game, I guess. Don't do it. Put it out of your mind. Take that medicine every two hours according to directions on the bottle and you'll be all right, my boy."

Don thanked him, slipped the prescription in a pocket and headed for school. But Tim grabbed him and faced him about. "You don't swallow the prescription, Donald," he said. "You take it to a druggist and he gives you something in a bottle. That's what you swallow, the stuff in the bottle. I'm not saying that it mightn't do you just as much good to eat the paper, but we'd better play by the rules. So come on, you lunk-head."

"Oh, I forgot," murmured Don.

"Of course you did," agreed the other sarcastically. "And, look here, if anyone asks you your name, it's Donald Croft Gilbert. Think you can remember that? Donald Croft——"

"Oh, dry up," said Don. "How much will this fool medicine cost me?"

"How much have you got?"

"About eighty cents, I think."

"It'll cost you eighty cents, then. Ask me something easier. I don't pretend to know how druggists do it, but they can always look right through your clothes and count your money. Never knew it to fail!"

But it failed this time, or else the druggist counted wrong, for the prescription was a dollar and Tim had to make up the balance. He insisted on Don taking the first dose then and there, so that he could get in another before bedtime, and Don meekly obeyed. After he had swallowed it he begged a glass of soda water from the druggist to take the taste out of his mouth, and the druggist, doubtless realising the demands of the occasion, stood treat to them both. On the way back Tim figured it that if they had only insisted on having ice-cream sodas they would have reduced the price of the medicine to its rightful cost. Don, though, firmly insisted that it was worth every cent of what he had paid for it.

"No one," he said convincedly, "could get that much nastiness into a small bottle for less than a dollar!"

CHAPTER XVII
DROPPED FROM THE TEAM

WHETHER owing to Danny Moore's tonic, the doctor's prescription or a good night's rest, Don awoke the next morning feeling perfectly well physically, and his first waking moments were cheered by the knowledge. Then, however, recollection of the fact that physical well-being was exactly what wasn't required under the circumstances brought quick reaction, and he jumped out of bed to look at himself in the mirror above his dresser in the hope of finding pale cheeks and hollow eyes and similar evidences of impending dissolution. But Fate had played a sorry trick on him! His cheeks were not in the least pale, nor were his eyes sunken. In short, he looked particularly healthy, and if other evidence of the fact was needed it was supplied by Tim. Tim, when Don turned regretfully away from the glass, was sitting up and observing him with pleased relief.

"Ata boy!" exclaimed Tim. "Feeling fine and dandy, aren't you? I guess that medicine was cheap at the price, after all! You look about a hundred per cent better than you did yesterday, Donald."

Don started to smile, caught himself in time and drew a long sigh. "You can't always tell by a fellow's looks how he's really feeling," he replied darkly.

"Oh, run away and play! What's the matter with you? You've got colour in your face and look great."

"Too much colour, I'm afraid," said Don, shaking his head pessimistically. "I guess—I guess I've got a little fever."

Tim stared at him puzzledly. "Fever? What for? I mean—— Say, are you fooling?"

"No. My face is sort of hot, honest, Tim." And so it was, possibly the consciousness of fibbing and the difficulty of doing it successfully was responsible for the flush. Tim pushed his legs out of bed and viewed his friend disgustedly.

"Don, you're getting to be one of those kleptomaniacs—no, that isn't it! What's the word? Hydrochondriacs, isn't it? Anyway, whatever it is, you're it! You've got so you imagine you're sick when you aren't. Forget it, Donald, and cheer up!"

"Oh, I'll be all right, thanks," responded the other dolefully. "I guess I'm lots better than I was."

"Of course you are! Why, hang it, man, you've simply got to be O. K. today! If you're not Robey'll can you as sure as shooting! Smile for the gentleman, Don, and then get a move on and come to breakfast."

"I don't think I want any breakfast, thanks."

"You will when you smell it. Want me to start the water for you?"

"If I was a hydrochondriac I wouldn't want any water, would I?"

"Hypochondriac's what I meant, I guess. Hurry up before the mob gets there."

Tim struggled into his bath-robe and pattered off down the corridor, leaving Don to follow at his leisure. But, instead of following, Don seated himself on the edge of his bed and viewed life gloomily. If Tim refused to believe in his illness, how was he to convince Coach Robey of it? He might, he reflected, rub talcum on his face, but he was afraid that wouldn't deceive anyone, the coach least of all. And, according to his bargain with Harry Walton, he must sever his connection with the team today. If he didn't Walton would go to the principal and tell what he had witnessed from his window that Saturday night, and not only he, but Tim and Clint as well, would suffer. And, still worse, the team would be beaten by Claflin as surely as—as Tim was shouting to him from the bathroom! He got up and donned his bath-robe and set off down the corridor with lagging feet, so wretched in mind by this time that it required no great effort of imagination to believe himself ailing in body.

To his surprise—and rather to his disgust—he found himself intensely hungry at breakfast and it was all he could do to refuse the steak and baked potato set before him. Under the appraising eye of Mr. Robey, he drank a glass of milk and nibbled at a piece of toast, his very soul longing for that steak and a couple of soft eggs! Afterward, when he reported to Danny, the trainer produced fresh discouragement in him.

"Fine, me boy!" declared the trainer. "You're as good as

90

ever, aren't you? Keep in the air all you can and go light with the dinner."

"I—I don't feel very fit," muttered Don.

"Get along with you! You're the picture of health! Don't be saying anything like that to Mr. Robey, or he might believe it and bench you. Run along now and mind what I tell you. Game's at two-fifteen today."

It was fortunate that Don had but two recitations that morning, for he was in no condition for such unimportant things. His mind was too full of what was before him. At dinner it was easy enough to obey Danny's command and eat lightly, for he was far too worried to want food. The noon meal was eaten early in order that the players might have an hour for digestion before they went to the field. Chambers came swinging up to the school at half-past one, in all the carriages to be found at the station, while her supporters trailed after on foot. The stands filled early and, by the time the Chambers warriors trotted on to the gridiron for their practice, looked gay and colourful with waving pennants.

Don kept close to Tim from the time dinner was over until they reached the locker-room in the gymnasium. Tim was puzzled and disgusted over his chum's behaviour and secretly began to think that perhaps, after all, he was not in the condition his appearance told him to be. Don listlessly dragged his playing togs on and was dressed by the time Coach Robey came in. He hoped that the coach would give him his opportunity then to declare his unfitness for work, but Mr. Robey paid no attention to him. He said the usual few words of admonition to the players, conferred with Manager Morton and the trainer and disappeared again. Captain Edwards led the way out of the building at a few minutes before two and they jogged down to the field and, heralded by a long cheer from the stand, took their places on the benches. It was a fine day for football, bright and windless and with a true November nip in the air.

Chambers yielded half the gridiron and Coach Robey approached the bench. "All right, first and second squads," he said cheerfully. "Try your signals out, but take it easy. Rollins, you'd better try a half-dozen goals. Martin, too. How about you, Gilbert? You feeling all right?"

Don felt the colour seeping out of his cheeks as the coach turned toward him, and there was an instant of silence before he replied with lowered eyes.

"N-no, sir, I'm not feeling very—very fit. I'm sorry."

"You're not?" Mr. Robey's voice had an edge. "Danny says you're perfectly fit. What's wrong?"

"I—I don't know, sir. I don't feel—well."

A number of the players still within hearing turned to listen. Mr. Robey viewed Don with a puzzled frown. Then he shrugged impatiently.

"You know best, of course," he said shortly, "but if you don't work today, Gilbert, you're plumb out of it. I can't keep your place open for you forever, you know. What do you say? Want to try it?"

Don wished that the earth under his feet would open up and swallow him. He tried to return the coach's gaze, but his eyes wandered. The first time he tried to speak he made no sound, and when he did find his voice it was so low that the coach impatiently bade him speak up.

"I don't think it would be any good, sir," replied Don huskily. "I—I'm not feeling very well."

There was a long silence. Then Mr. Robey's voice came to him as cold as ice. "Very well, Gilbert, clean your locker out and hand in your things to the trainer. Walton!"

"Yes, sir?"

"Go in at left guard on the first squad." Mr. Robey turned again to Don. "Gilbert," he said very quietly, "I don't understand you. You are perfectly able to play, and you know it. The only explanation that occurs to me is that you're in a funk. If that's so it is a fortunate thing for all of us that we've discovered it now instead of later. There's no place on this team, my boy, for a quitter."

Coach and players turned away, leaving Don standing alone there before the bench. Miserably he groped his way to it and sat down with hanging head. His eyes were wet and he was horribly afraid that someone would see it. A hand fell on his shoulder and he glanced up into Tim's troubled face.

"I heard, Don," said Tim. "I'm frightfully sorry, old man. Are you sure you can't do it!"

Don shook his head silently. Tim sighed.

"Gee, it's rotten, ain't it? Maybe he didn't mean what he said, though. Maybe, if you're all right Monday, he'll give you another chance. I'm—I'm beastly sorry, Don!"

The hand on his shoulder pressed reassuringly and drew away and Tim hurried out to his place. Presently Don took a deep breath, got to his feet and, trying his hardest to look unconcerned but making sorry work of it, skirted the stand and retraced his steps to the gymnasium. His one desire was to get out of sight before any of the fellows found him, and so he pulled off his togs as quickly as he

92

might, got into his other clothes, made a bundle of his suit and stockings and shoes and left them in the rubbing-room where Danny could not fail to find them and then hurried out of the building and through the deserted yard to Billings and the sunlit silence and emptiness of his room.

There was very little consolation in the knowledge that he had done only what was right. Martyrdom has its drawbacks. He had lost his position with the team and had been publicly branded a quitter. The fact that his conscience was not only clear but even approving didn't help much. Being thought a quitter, a coward, hurt badly. If he could have got at Harry Walton any time during the ensuing half-hour it would have gone hard with that youth. After a time, though, he got command of his feelings again and, since there was nothing better to do, he seated himself at the window and watched as much of the football game as was visible from there. Once or twice he was able to forget his trouble for a brief moment.

Chambers put up a good game that day and it was all the home team could do to finally win out by the score of 3 to 0. For two periods Chambers had Brimfield virtually on the run, and only a fine fighting spirit that flashed into evidence under the shadow of her goal saved the latter from defeat. As it was, luck took a hand in matters when a poor pass from centre killed Chambers's chance of scoring by a field-goal in the second quarter.

Brimfield showed better work in the second half and twice got the ball inside the visitor's twenty-yard line, once in the third period and again shortly before the final whistle blew. The first opportunity to score was lost when Carmine called for line-plunges to get the pigskin across and Howard, who was playing in St. Clair's position because of a slight injury to the regular left half, fumbled for a four-yard loss. Chambers rallied and took the ball away a minute later. In the fourth period dazzling runs outside of tackles by Tim Otis and hard line-plugging by Rollins and Howard took the ball from Brimfield's thirty-five to the enemy's twenty-five. There a forward pass grounded—Chambers had a remarkable defence against that play—and, on third down, Rollins slid off left tackle for enough to reach the twenty. But with only one down remaining and time nearly up, a try-at-goal was the only course left, and Rollins, standing squarely on the thirty-yard line, drop-kicked a scanty victory.

In some ways that contest was disappointing, in others encouraging. Team-play was more in evidence than in any previous game and the maroon-and-grey backfield had performed prodigiously. And the plays had, as a general thing, gone off like clock-work. But there were weak places in the line still. Pryme, at right guard, had proved an easy victim for the enemy and the same was true, in a lesser degree, of Harry Walton, on the other side of centre. And Crewe, at right tackle, had allowed himself to be boxed time after time. It might be said for Crewe, however, that today he was playing opposite an opponent who was more than clever. But the way in which Chambers had torn holes in Brimfield's first defence promised poorly for next Saturday and the spectators went away from the field feeling a bit less sanguine than a week before. "No team that is weak at both guard positions can hope to win," was the general verdict, and it was fully realised that Claflin's backs were better than Chambers's. For a day or two there was much talk of a petition to the faculty asking for the reinstatement of Tom Hall, but it progressed no further than talk. Josh, it was known, was not the kind to reverse his decision for any reason they could present.

And yet, although the weekly faculty conference on Monday night had no written petition to consider, the subject of Tom's reinstatement did come before it and in a totally unprecedented manner.

CHAPTER XVIII
"GOOD-BYE, TIMMY!"

TIM found a dejected and most unsatisfactory chum when he got back to the room after the Chambers game that Saturday afternoon. All of Tim's demands for an explanation of the whole puzzling affair met only with evasion. Don was not only uncommunicative, but a trifle short-tempered, a condition quite unusual for him. All Tim could get from him was that he "felt perfectly punk" and wasn't going to try to change Mr. Robey's decision.

"I'm through," he said. "I don't blame Robey a bit. I'm no use on the team as I am. He'd be foolish to bother with me."

"Well, all I can say," returned Tim, with a sigh of exasperation, "is that the whole thing is mighty funny. I guess there's more to it than you're telling. You look like thirty cents, all right enough, but I'll wager anything you like that you could go out there and play just as good a game as ever on Monday if Robey would let you and you cared to try. Now couldn't you!"

"I don't know. What does it matter, anyhow? I tell you I'm all through, and so there's no use chewing it over."

"Oh, all right. Nuff said." Tim walked to the window, his hands thrust deep in his pockets, and, after a minute's contemplation of the darkening prospect without, observed haltingly: "Look here, Don. If you hear things you don't like, don't get up on your ear, eh?"

"What sort of things?" demanded the other.

Tim hesitated a long moment before he took the plunge. Then: "Well, some of the fellows don't understand, Don. You can't altogether blame them, I suppose. I shut two or three of them up, but there's bound to be some talk, you know. Some fellows always manage to think of the meanest things possible. But what fellows like that say isn't worth bothering about. So just you sit snug, old man. They've already found that they can't say that sort of thing when I'm around."

"Thanks," said Don quietly. "What sort of things do you mean?"

"Oh, anything."

"You mean that they're calling me a quitter?"

"Well, some of them heard Robey get that off and they're repeating it like a lot of silly parrots. I called Holt down good and hard. Told him I'd punch his ugly face if he talked that way again."

"Don't bother," said Don listlessly. "I guess I do look like a quitter, all right."

"Piffle! And, hang it all, Robey had no business saying that, Don! He couldn't really believe it."

"Why couldn't he? On the face of it, Tim, I'd say that I looked a whole lot like a quitter."

"But that's nonsense! Why would you or any fellow want to quit just before the Claflin game? Why, all the hard work's done with, man! Only a little signal practice to go through with now. Why would you want to quit? It's poppycock!"

"Well, some fellows do get cold feet just before the big game. We've both known cases of it. Look at——"

"Yes, I know what you're going to say, but that was different. He never had any spunk, anyway. Nobody believed in him but Robey, and Robey was wrong, just as he is about you. Anyway, all I'm trying to say is that there's no use getting waxy if some idiot shoots off his mouth. The fellows who really count don't believe you a—a quitter. And the whole business will blow over in a couple of days. Look how they talked about Tom at first!"

"They didn't call him a quitter, though. They were just mad

because he'd done a fool thing and lost the team. I wouldn't blame anyone for thinking me a—a coward, and I can't resent it if they say it."

"Can't, eh? Well, I can!"

Don smile wanly. "Thought you were telling me not to, Tim."

Tim muttered. There was silence for a minute in the twilit room. Then Tim switched on the lights and rolled up his sleeves preparatory to washing. "The whole thing's perfectly rotten," he growled, "but we'll just have to make the best of it. Ten years from now——"

"Yes, but it isn't ten years from now that troubles me," interrupted Don thoughtfully. "It—it's right this minute. And tomorrow and the next day. And the day after that. I've a good mind to——"

"To what?" demanded Tim from behind his sponge.

"Nothing. I was just—thinking."

"Well, stop it, then. You weren't intended to think. You always do something silly when you get to thinking. Wash up and come on to supper."

"I'm not going over tonight," answered Don. "I'm not hungry. And, anyway, I don't feel quite like facing it yet."

"Now, look here," began Tim severely, "if you're going to take it like that——"

"I'm not, I guess. Only I'd rather not go to supper tonight. I am through at the training-table and I funk going back to the other table just now. Besides, I'm not the least bit hungry. You run along."

Tim observed him frowningly. "Well, all right. Only if it was me I'd take the bull by the horns and see it through. Fellows will talk more if you let them see that you give a hang."

"They'll talk enough anyway, I dare say. A little more won't matter."

"I just hope Holt gets gay again," said Tim venomously, shying the towel in the general direction of the rack and missing it by a foot. "Want me to bring something over to you?"

"No, thanks. I don't want a thing."

"We-ell, I guess I'll beat it then." Tim loitered uncertainly at the door. "I say, Donald, old scout, buck up, eh?"

"Oh, yes, I'll be all right, Timmy. Don't you worry about me. And—and thanks, you know, for—for calling Holt down."

"Oh, that!" Tim chuckled. "Holt wasn't the only one I called down either." Then, realising that he had not helped the situation any by the remark, he tried to squirm out of it. "Of course, Holt was

96

the one, you know. The others didn't really say anything, or—or mean anything——"

Don laughed. "That'll do, Tim. Beat it!"

And Tim, red-faced and confused, "beat it."

For the next five minutes doors in the corridor opened and shut and footfalls sounded as the fellows hurried off to Wendell. But I doubt if Don heard the sounds, for he was sunk very low in the chair and his eyes were fixed intently on space. Presently he drew in his legs, sat up and pulled his watch from his pocket. A moment of speculation followed. Then he jumped from the chair as one whose mind is at last made up and went to his closet. From the recesses he dragged forth his bag and laid it open on his bed. From the closet hooks he took down a few garments and tossed them beside the bag and then crossed to his dresser and pulled open the drawers. Don had decided to accept Coach Robey's title. He was going to quit!

There was a train at six-thirty-four and another at seven-one for New York. With luck, he could get the first. If he missed that he was certain of the second. The dormitory was empty, it was quite dark outside by now and there was scarcely a chance of anyone's seeing him. If he hurried he could be at the station before Tim could return from supper. Or, even if he didn't get away until the seven-one train, he would be clear of the hall before Tim could discover his absence and surmise the reason for it. To elude Tim was the all-important thing, for Tim would never approve and would put all sorts of obstacles in his way. In fact, it would be a lot like Tim to hold him back by main force! Don's heart sank for a moment. It was going to be frightfully hard to leave old Timmy. Perhaps they might meet again at college in a couple of years, but they would not be likely to see each other before that time, and even that depended on so many things that it couldn't be confidently counted on.

Don paused in his hurried selection of articles from the dresser drawers and dropped into a chair at the table. But, with the pad before him and pen in hand, he shook his head. A note would put Tim wise to what was happening and perhaps allow him to get to the station in time to make a fuss. No, it would be better to write to him later; perhaps from New York tonight, for Don was pretty sure that he wouldn't be able to get a through train before morning. So, with another glance at his watch, he began to pack again, throwing things in every which-way in his feverish desire to complete the task and leave the building before Tim got back. He came across a scarf that Tim had admired and laid it back in the top drawer. It had never been worn and Tim should have it. And as he hurried back and forth he thought of other things he would like Tim to have. There was his tennis racket, the one Tim always borrowed when Don wasn't using it, and a scarf-pin made of a queer, rough nugget of opal matrix. He would tell Tim he was to have those and not to pack them with the other things. The thought of making the gifts almost cheered him for awhile, and, together with the excitement of running away, caused him to hum a little tune under his breath as he jammed the last articles in the bag and snapped it shut.

It was sixteen minutes past now. He would, he acknowledged, never be able to make the six-thirty-four, with that burden to carry. But the seven-one would do quite as well, and he wouldn't have to hurry so. In that case, then, why not leave just a few words of good-bye for Tim? He could put the note somewhere where Tim wouldn't find it until later; tuck it, for instance, under the bed-clothes so that he would find it when he pulled them down. He hesitated a moment and then set his bag down by the door, dropped his overcoat and umbrella on the bed and seated himself again at the table. Tim was never known to take less than a half-hour for supper and he still had a good ten minutes' leeway:

"Dear Timmy [he wrote hurriedly], I'm off. It's no use sticking around any longer. Fellows aren't going to forget as soon as you said and I can't stay on here and be thought a quitter. So I'm taking the seven-one to New York and will be home day after tomorrow. I wish you would pack my things up for me when you get time. There isn't any great hurry. I've got enough for awhile. You're to keep the racket and the blue and white tie and the opal matrix pin and anything else you like to remember me by. Please do this, Tim. I'll write from home and tell you about sending the trunk. I'm awfully sorry, Tim, and I'm going to miss you like anything, but I shan't ever come back here. Maybe we will get together again at college. I hope so. You try, will you? Good-bye, Tim, old pal. We've had some dandy times together, haven't we? And you've been an A1 chum to me and I wish I wasn't going off without saying good-bye to you decently. But I've got to. So good-bye, Timmy, old man. Think of me now and then like I will of you. Good-bye.

"Your friend always, "DON."

That note took longer to write than he had counted on, and when he got up from the table and looked at his watch he was alarmed to find that it was almost half-past six. He folded the paper and tucked it just under the clothes at the head of Tim's bed, took a last glance about the room, picked up coat and umbrella and turned out the light. Then he strode toward the door, groping for his bag.

CHAPTER XIX
FRIENDS FALL OUT

TIM didn't enjoy supper very much that evening. The game had left him pretty weary of body and mind, and on top of that was Don and his trouble, and try as he might he couldn't get them out of his thoughts. Mr. Robey was not at table; someone said he had gone to New York for over Sunday; and so Tim didn't have to make a pretence of eating more than he wanted. And he wanted very little. A slice of cold roast beef, rather too rare to please him, about an eighth of one of the inevitable baked potatoes, a few sips of milk and a corner of a slice of toast as hard as a shingle, and Tim was more than satisfied. Tonight he was not especially interested in the talk, which, as usual after a game, was all football, and didn't see any good reason for sitting there after he had finished and listening to it. All during his brief meal he was on the alert for any mention of Don's name, and more than once he glared, almost encouragingly, at Holt. But Holt had already learned his lesson and was doing very little talking, and none at all about Don. Nor was the absent player's name mentioned by anyone at that table, although what might be being said of him at the other Tim had no way of knowing. He stayed on a few minutes after he had finished, eyeing the apple-sauce and graham crackers coldly, and then asked Steve Edwards to excuse him.

"Off his feed," remarked Carmine as Tim passed down the dining hall on his way out. "First time I ever saw old Tim have nerves."

"It's Don Gilbert, probably," said Clint Thayer. "They're great pals. Tim's worried about him, I guess."

"What do you make of it, Steve?" asked Crewe, helping himself to a third slice of meat.

"What is there to make of it?" asked Steve carelessly. "The chap's all out of shape, I suppose. I don't know what his trouble is, but I guess he's a goner for this year."

"It's awfully funny, isn't it?" asked Rollins. "Gilbert always struck me as an awfully plucky player."

"Has anyone said he isn't?" inquired Clint quietly.

"N-no, no, of course not!" Rollins flushed. "I didn't mean anything like that, Clint. Only I don't see——"

"He hasn't been looking very fit lately," offered Harry Walton. "I noticed it two or three days ago. Too bad!"

"Yes, you're feeling perfectly wretched about it, I guess," said big Thursby drily, causing a smile around the table. Walton shrugged and rewarded the speaker with one of his smiles that were always unfortunately like leers.

"Oh, I can feel sorry for him," said Walton, "even if I do get his place. Gilbert gave me an awfully good fight for it."

"Oh, was there a fight?" asked Thursby innocently. "I didn't notice any."

Thursby got a real laugh this time and Harry Walton joined in to save his face, but with no very good grace.

"If anyone has an idea that Don Gilbert is scared and quit for that reason," observed St. Clair, "he'd better keep it to himself. Or, anyhow, he'd better not air it when Tim is about. He nearly bit my head off in the gym because I said that Don was a chump to give up like this a week before the Claflin game. Tim flared up like—like a gasoline torch and wanted to fight! I didn't mean a thing by my innocent remark, but I had the dickens of a time trying to prove it to Tim! And he almost jumped into you, too, didn't he, Holt?"

"Yes, he did, the touchy beggar! You all heard what Robey said, and——"

"I didn't hear," interrupted Steve, "and——"

"Why, he said——"

"And, as I was about to remark, Holt, I don't want to. And it will be just as decent for those who did hear to forget. Robey says lots of things he doesn't mean or believe. Perhaps that was one of them. I'm for Don. If he says he's sick, he is sick. You've all seen him play for two years and you ought to know that there isn't a bit of yellow anywhere in his make-up."

"That's so," agreed several, and others nodded, Holt amongst them.

"I didn't say he was a quitter, Steve. I was only repeating what Robey said, and Tim happened to hear me. Gee, I like Don as well as any of you. Gee, didn't I play a whole year with him on the second?"

"Gee, you did indeed!" replied Crewe, and, laughing, the fellows pushed back their chairs and left the table.

Tim didn't hurry on his way along the walk to Billings, for he was earnestly trying to think of some scheme that would take Don's mind off his trouble that evening. Perhaps he could get Don to take a good, long walk. Walking always worked wonders in his own case when, as very infrequently happened, he had a fit of the blues. Yes, he would propose a walk, he told himself. And then he groaned at the thought of it, for he was very tired and he ached in a large number of places!

Only a few windows were lighted in Billings as he approached it, for most of the fellows were still in dining hall and the rule requiring the turning out of lights during absence from rooms was strictly enforced. Only the masters were exempted, and Tim noticed as he passed Mr. Daley's study that the droplight was turned low by one of those cunning dimming attachments which Tim had always envied the instructor the possession of. Tim would have had one of those long ago could he have put it to any practical use. He passed through the doorway and down the dimly lighted corridor, the rubber-soled shoes which he affected in all seasons making little sound. He was surprised to see that no light showed through the transom of Number 6, and he paused outside the door a moment. Perhaps Don was asleep. In that case, it would be just as well to not disturb him. But, on the other hand, he might be just sitting there in the dark being miserable. Tim turned the knob and pushed the door open.

The light from the corridor and the fact that Don had stopped startledly at the sound of the turning knob prevented an actual collision between them. Tim, pushing the door slowly shut behind him, viewed Don questioningly. "Hello," he said, "where are you going?"

"For a walk," replied Don.

"Why the coat and umbrella? And—oh, I see!" Tim's glance took in the bag and comprehension dawned. "So that's it, eh?"

There was an instant of silence during which Tim closed the door and leaned against it, hands in pockets and a thoughtful scowl on his face. Finally:

"Yes, that's it," said Don defiantly. "I'm off for home."

"What's the big idea?"

"You know well enough, Tim. I—I'm not going to stay here and be—be pointed out as a quitter. I'm——"

"Wait a sec! What are you doing now but quitting, you several sorts of a blind mule? Think you're helping things any by—by running away? Don't be a chump, Donald."

"That's all well enough for you. It isn't your funeral. I don't care what they say about me if I don't have to hear it. I'm sorry, Tim, but—but I've just got to do it. I—there's a note for you in your bed. I didn't expect you'd be back before I left."

"I'll bet you didn't, son!" said Tim grimly. "Now let me tell you something, Don. You're acting like a baby, that's what you're doing! It's all fine enough to say that you don't care what fellows say as long as you don't hear it, but you don't mean it, Don. You would care. And so would I. If you don't want them to think you a quitter, for the love of mud don't run away like—like one!"

"I've thought of all that, Tim, but it's the only thing to do."

"The only thing to do, your grandmother! The thing to do is to stick around and show folks that you're not a quitter. Don't you see that getting out is the one thing that'll make them believe Robey was right?"

"Oh, I dare say, but I've made up my mind, Tim. I'm going to get that seven-one train, old man, and I'll have to beat it. If you want to walk along to the station with me——"

"And carry your bag?" asked Tim sweetly. He turned the key in the lock and then dropped it in his pocket. Don took a stride forward, but was met by Tim's challenging frown. "There's no seven-one train for you tonight, Donald," said Tim quietly, "nor any other night. Put your bag down, old dear, and hang your overcoat back in the closet."

"Don't act like a silly ass," begged Don. "Put that key back and let me out, Tim!"

"Yes, I will—like fun! The only way you'll get that key will be by taking it out of my pocket, and by the time you do that the seven-one train will be half-way to the city."

"Please, Tim! You're not acting like a good chum! Just you think——"

"That's just what I am acting like," returned Tim, stepping past the other and switching on the lights. "And you'll acknowledge it tomorrow. Just now you're sort of crazy in the head. I'll humour you as much as possible, Donald, but not to the extent of letting you make a perfect chump of yourself. Sit down and behave."

"Tim, I want that key," said Don sternly.

Tim shrugged. "Can't have it, Don, unless you fight for it. And I'm not sure you'd get it then. Now look here——"

"You've no right to keep me here!"

"I don't give a hang whether I've got the right or not. You're going to stay here."

"There are other trains," said Don coldly. "You can't keep that door locked forever."

"I don't intend to try, but it'll stay locked until the last train tonight has whistled for the crossing back there. Make up your mind to that, son!"

Don looked irresolutely from Tim to the door and back again. He didn't want to fight Tim the least bit in the world. He wasn't so sure now that he wanted to get that train, either. But, having stated his purpose, he felt it encumbent on him to carry it out. Then his gaze fell on the windows and he darted toward them.

But Tim had already thought of that way of escape and before Don had traversed half the distance from door to windows Tim had planted himself resolutely in the way. "No you don't, Donald," he said calmly. "You'll have to lick me first, boy, and I'm feeling quite some scrappy!"

"I don't want to lick you," said Don irritably, "but I mean to get that train. You'd better either give up that key or stand out of my way, Tim."

"Neither, thanks. And, look here, if we get to scrapping Horace will hear us and then you won't get away in any case. Be sensible, Don, and give it up. It can't be done, old man."

"Will you unlock that door?" demanded Don angrily.

"No, confound you, I won't!"

"Then I'm going out by the window!"

"And I say you're not." Tim swiftly peeled off his coat. "Anyway, not in time to get that train."

Don dropped his bag to the floor and tossed overcoat and umbrella on his bed. "I've given you fair warning, Tim," he said in a low voice. "I don't want to hurt you, but you'd better stand aside."

"I don't want to get hurt, Don," replied the other quietly, "but if you insist, all right. I'm doing what I'd want you to do, Don, if I went crazy in the head. You may not like it now, but some day you'll tell me I did right."

"You're acting like a fool," answered Don hotly. "It's no business of yours if I want to get out of here. Now you let me pass, or it'll be the worse for you!"

"Don, will you listen to reason? Sit down calmly for five minutes and let's talk this thing over. Will you do that?"

"No! And I won't be dictated to by you, Tim Otis! Now get out of the way!"

"You'll have to put me out," answered Tim with set jaw. "And you're going to find that hard work, Donald. We're both going to get horribly mussed up, and——"

But Tim didn't finish his remark, for at that instant Don rushed him. Tim met the onslaught squarely and in a second they were struggling silently. No blows were struck. Don was bent only on getting the other out of the way and making his escape through the open window there, while Tim was equally resolved that he should do nothing of the sort. In spite of Don's superior weight, the two boys were fairly equally matched, and for a minute or two they strained and tussled without advantage to either. Then Tim, his arms wrapped around Don's body like iron bands, forced the latter back a step and against a chair which went crashing to the floor. Don tore at the encircling arms, panting.

"I don't—want to—hurt you," he muttered, "but—I will—if you don't—let go!"

There was no answer from Tim, but the grip didn't relax. Don worked a hand under the other's chin and tried to force his head back. Tim gave a little and they collided with the window-seat, stumbled and slid together to the floor, Don on top. For a moment they writhed and thrashed and then Don worked his right arm loose, slowly tore Tim's left hand away and held it down to the floor.

"Let go or I'll punch you, Tim," he panted.

"Punch—ahead!"

Don strained until he felt Tim's other hand giving, and then, with a sudden fling of his body, rolled clear and jumped to his feet. But Tim was only an instant behind him and, panting and dishevelled, the two boys confronted each other, silent.

"I'm going out there," said Don after a moment.

Tim only shook his head and smiled crookedly.

"I am, Tim, and—and you mustn't try to stop me this time!"

"I've—got to, Don!"

"I'm giving you fair warning!"

"I know."

Don took a deeper breath and stepped forward. "Don't touch me!" he warned. But Tim was once more in his path, hands stretched to clutch and hold. "Out of my way, Tim! Fair warning!" Don's face was white and his eyes blazing.

"No!" whispered Tim, and crouched.

Then Don went on again. Tim threw himself in the way, a fist shot out and Tim, with a grunt, went back against the pillows and slipped heavily to the floor.

Don's hands fell to his sides and he stared bewilderedly. Then, with a groan, he dropped to his knees and raised Tim's head from the floor. "Gee, but I'm sorry, Timmy!" he stammered. "I didn't mean to do it, honest! I was crazy, I guess! Timmy, are you all right!"

Tim's eyes, half-closed, fluttered, he drew a deep breath and his head rolled over against Don's arm.

"Timmy!" cried Don anxiously. "Timmy! Don't you hear me! I didn't hit you awfully hard, Timmy!"

Tim sighed. "What—time is it?" he murmured.

"Time? Never mind the time. Are you all right, Tim?"

Tim opened his eyes and grinned weakly. "Hear the birdies sing, Don! It was a lovely punch! Help me up, will you?"

Don lifted him to the window-seat. "I'm horribly sorry, Tim," he said abjectedly. "I—I didn't know what I was doing, chum! I wish—I wish you'd hand me one, Tim! Go on, will you?"

Tim laughed weakly. "It's all right, Donald. Just give me a minute to get my breath. Gee, things certainly spun around there for a second!"

"Where'd I hit you?"

"Right on the point of the jaw." Tim felt of the place gingerly. "No harm done, though. It just sort of—jarred me a bit. What time is it?"

Don glanced at the tin alarm clock on his dresser. "Ten of seven," he answered. "What's that got to do with it?"

"Well, you can't make the seven-one now, Donald, unless you fly all the way, can you?"

"Oh!" said Don, rather blankly. "I—I'd forgotten!"

"Good thing," muttered Tim. "Wish you'd forgotten before! If anyone ever tells you you're a nice good-natured, even-tempered chap, Don, don't you believe him. You send 'em to me!"

"I didn't know I could lose my temper like that," replied the other shamefacedly. "Timmy, I'm most awfully sorry about it. You believe that, don't you?"

"Sure!" Tim laughed. "But I'll bet you're not half as sorry as you would have been tomorrow if I'd let you go! Don, you're an awful ass, now aren't you?"

Don nodded. "I guess I am, Timmy. And you're a—a brick, old man!"

"Huh! Any more trains to New York tonight?"

"There's one at twelve-something," answered Don, with a grin.

"Thinking of catching it?"

"Not a bit!"

"All right then." Tim dug in his pocket and then tossed the door-key beside him on the cushion. "Better unpack your bag, you silly ass. Then we'll go out and get some air. I sort of need it!"

Some three hours later Tim, tossing back his bed-clothes, exclaimed: "Hello! What have we here?"

"That's just a note I wrote you," said Don hurriedly. "Hand it here, Tim."

"I should say not! I'm going to read it!"

"No, please, Tim! It's just about two or three things I was going to leave you! Hand it over, like a good chap!"

"Something you were going to leave me?" said Tim as he let

Don wrest the sheet of paper from him. "Oh, I see. Well,"—he felt carefully of the lump on his chin—"I guess you left me enough as it is, dearie!"

CHAPTER XX
AMY APPEARS FOR THE DEFENCE

PRACTICE on Monday was a wretched affair. To be sure, many of the fellows who had played in the Chambers game had been excused, but that didn't account for the fact that those who did take part went at their work as if half asleep. Both McPhee and Cotter failed to get any life into the first, and the second, while it, too, seemed to have taken part in the general slump, managed to score twice while the first was with difficulty wresting three touchdowns from its opponent. Mr. Robey shouted himself red in the face, Steve Edwards, who followed practice, pleaded and exhorted, and a stocky, broad-shouldered, bearded individual who made his appearance that afternoon for the first time frowned and shook his head, and all to small purpose. The players accepted scoldings and insults as a donkey accepts blows, untroubledly, apathetically, and jogged on at their own pace, guilty of all the sins of commission and omission in the football decalogue.

There was much curiosity about the newcomer and many opinions as to his identity were hazarded on the bench that afternoon. It was quite evident that he was a football authority, for Coach Robey consulted him at times all during practice. And it was equally evident that they were close friends, since the stranger was on one occasion seen to smite the head coach most familiarly between the shoulders! But who he was and what he was doing there remained a secret until after supper. Then it became known that his name was Proctor, Doctor George G. Proctor, that he was a practising physician some place in the Middle West and that he was visiting Coach Robey. But that was unsatisfactory data and some enterprising youth hunted back in the football records and, lo, the mystery was explained. Eight years before "Gus" Proctor had played tackle on the Princeton eleven and in his junior and senior years had been honoured with a position on the All-American Team. Subsequently he had coached at a college in Ohio and had put said college on the map. Now, having stolen away from home to see

Princeton and Yale play next Saturday, he was staying for a day or two with Mr. Robey. After that became generally known Doctor Proctor was gazed at with a new respect whenever he appeared on field or campus.

Don and Tim went up to Number 12 that night after supper to call on Tom Hall. Tim was having hard work making Don face the music. If Don could have had his way he would have kept to himself, but Tim insisted on dragging him around. "Just keep a firm upper lip, Donald," he counselled, "and show the fellows that there's nothing in it. That's the only way to do. If you keep skulking off by yourself they'll think you're ashamed."

"So I am," muttered Don.

"You're not, either! You've done nothing to be ashamed of! Keep that in mind, you silly It. Now come along and we'll go up and jolly Tom a bit."

Steve Edwards was not at home, but Amy Byrd was enthroned on the window-seat when they entered in response to Tom's invitation, and Amy had evidently been holding forth very seriously on some subject.

"Don't mind us," said Tim. "Go ahead, Amy, and get it off your chest."

"Hello," said Amy. "Hello, Don, old man. Haven't seen you for an age. Make yourselves at home. Never mind Tom, he's only the host. How did you like the practice today, Tim?"

"I didn't see it, but I heard enough about it. It must have been fierce!"

"It was perfectly punk," growled Tom. "I should think Robey would want to throw up his hands and quit!"

"Did you see it, Don?" asked Amy.

"No, I didn't go over. What was the trouble?"

"Well, I'm no expert," replied Amy, taking his knees into his arms and rocking gently back and forth on the seat, "but I'd say in my ignorant way that someone had unkindly put sleeping-potions in the milk at training-table! The only fellow who seemed to have his eyes more than half open was McPhee. Mac showed signs of life at long intervals. The rest sort of stumbled around in their sleep. I think Peters actually snored."

"Oh, we're going to get a fine old drubbing next Saturday," said Tom pessimistically. "And what a fine exhibition for that chap Proctor! I'll bet Robey could have kicked the whole team all the way back to the gym. He looked as though it would have done him a world of good to have a try at it!"

"Oh, well, these things happen," said Tim cheerfully. "It's only a slump. We'll get over it."

"Slump be blowed!" said Tom. "This is a fine time to slump, five days before the game!"

"I know that, too, but there's no use howling about it. What we need, Tom, is to have you get back there at right guard, old man."

"That's what I've been saying," exclaimed Amy earnestly. "I want Tom to go to Josh and ask him to let him play, but he won't. Says it wouldn't be any good. You don't know whether it would or not, Tom, until you try it. Look here, Josh doesn't want us to get beaten Saturday any more than we want it ourselves, and if you sort of put it up to him like that——"

"I'd look well, wouldn't I?" laughed Tom. "Telling Josh that unless he let me off pro the team would get licked! Gee, that's some modest, isn't it?"

"You don't have to put it like that," replied Amy impatiently. "Be—be diplomatic. Tell him——"

"What we ought to do," interrupted Tim, "is get up a petition and have everyone sign it."

"I thought of that, too," said Amy, "but this dunder-headed Turk won't stand for even that."

"Why not, Tom?" asked Don.

"Because."

"And after that?" asked Amy sweetly.

"Well, look here, you chaps." Tom scowled intently for a moment. "Look here. It's this way. Josh put a bunch of us on pro, didn't he? Well, what right have I to go and ask to be let off just because I happen to be a football man? You don't suppose those other fellows like it any better than I do, do you?"

"Oh, forget that! I'm one of them, and I'm having the time of my life. It's been the making of me, Tom. I'm getting so blamed full of learning that I'll be able to loaf all the rest of the year; live on my income, so to say." And Amy beamed proudly.

"That's all right," answered Tom doggedly, "but I don't intend to cry-baby. I'm just as much in it as any of you. If Josh wants to let us all off, all right, but I'm not going to ask for a—a special dispensation!"

"You don't need to," said Tim. "Let the fellows do it. That has nothing to do with you. What's to keep us from going ahead and getting up a petition?"

"Because I ask you not to," replied Tom simply. "It's only fair that we should all be punished alike."

"But you're not," said Don.

108

"We're not? Why aren't we?" asked Tom in surprise.

"Because you're getting it harder than Amy and Harry Westcott and the others," answered Don quietly. "They aren't barred from any sport, and you are."

"By Jove, that's a fact!" exclaimed Amy.

"But—but we all got the same sentence," protested Tom.

"I know you did, but"—Don smiled—"put it like this. I hate parsnips; can't bear them. Suppose you and I were punished for something we'd done by being made to eat parsnips three times a day for—for a month! You like them, don't you? Well, who'd get the worst of that? The sentence would be the same, but the—the punishment would be a heap worse for me, wouldn't it?"

"'Father was right'!" said Tim.

"Oh, father never spoke a truer word!" cried Amy, jumping up from the window-seat. "That settles it, Tom! Get some paper, Tim, and we'll write that petition this minute and I'll guarantee to get fifty signatures before ten o'clock!"

"You'll do nothing of the sort," said Tom stubbornly. "Don talks like a lawyer, all right, but he's all wrong. And, anyway, I'm out of football and I'm going to stay out for this year. I've quit training and I probably couldn't play if Josh said I might. So that——"

"Oh, piffle," said Amy. "Quit training! Everyone knows you never quit training, Tom. You could go out there tomorrow and play as good a game as you ever did. Don't talk like a sick duck!"

"There's no reason why I should play, though. Pryme's putting up a bully game——"

"Pryme is doing the best he knows how," said Tim, "but Pryme can't play guard as you can, Tom, and he never will, and you know it! Now have a grain of sense, won't you? Just sit tight and let us put this thing through. There isn't a fellow in school who won't be tickled to death to sign that petition, and I'll bet you anything you like that Josh will be just as tickled to say yes to it. Whatever you say about Josh Fernald, you've got to hand it to him for being fair and square, Tom."

"Josh is all right, sure. I haven't said anything against him, have I? But I won't stand for any petition, fellows, so you might as well get that out of your heads. Besides, my being on the team or off it isn't going to make a half of one per cent's difference next Saturday."

There was silence in the room for a moment. Then Amy went dejectedly back to the window-seat and threw himself on it at full length. "I think you might, Tom," he said finally, "if only on my account!"

"Why on your account?" laughed Tom.

"Because I'm the guy that got you all into the mess, that's why. And I've felt good and mean about it ever since. And now, when we think up a perfectly good way to—to undo the mischief I made, you act like a mule. Think what a relief it would be to my conscience, Tom, if you got off pro and went back and played against Claflin!"

"I don't care a continental about your conscience, Amy. In fact I never knew before that you had one!"

"I've got a very nice one, thanks. It's well-trained, too. It——" Amy's voice trailed off into silence and for the next five minutes or so he took no part in the conversation, but just laid on the cushions and stared intently at the ceiling. Then, suddenly, he thumped his feet to the floor and reached for his cap.

"What time is it?" he demanded.

"Most eight," said Tim. "We'd better beat it."

"What time——" began Amy. Then he stopped, pulled his cap on his head and literally hurled himself across the room and through the door, leaving the others to gaze at each other amazedly.

"Well, what's wrong with him?" gasped Tim.

"He's got something in that crazy head of his," answered Tom uneasily. "Don't let him start that petition business, Tim, will you? I don't want to seem mean or anything, you know, but I'd rather let things be as they are. Come up again, fellows. And maybe today's showing doesn't mean anything, Tim, just as you said. We'll hope so, eh?"

Faculty conferences took place on Monday evenings at half-past seven in the faculty meeting room in Main Hall. At such times, with the principal, Mr. Fernald, presiding at the end of the long table and all members of the faculty able to attend ranged on either side, all and sundry matters pertaining to the government of the school came up for discussion. The business portion of the conference was followed by an informal half-hour of talk, during which many of the students were subjected to a dissection that would have surprised them vastly had they known of it. Tonight, however, the executive session was still going on and Mr. Brooke, the secretary, was still making notes at the foot of the table, when there came a rap at the door.

Mr. Fernald nodded to Mr. Brooke. "See who it is, please," he said.

The secretary laid down his pen very carefully on the clean square of blue blotting-paper before him, pushed back his chair and opened the door a few inches. When he turned around his countenance expressed a sort of pained disapprobation. "It's Byrd, sir," announced Mr. Brooke in a low, shocked voice. "He says he'd like to speak to you."

"Byrd? Well, tell him I'm busy," replied the principal. "If he wants to wait I'll see him after the conference. Although"—Mr. Fernald glanced at the clock—"it's only four minutes to eight and he'd better get back to his room. Tell him I'll see him at the Cottage at nine, Mr. Brooke. As I was saying," and Mr. Fernald faced the company again, "I think it would be well to arrange for a longer course this Winter. Last year, as you'll recall—— Eh? What is it?"

"He says, sir, that it's a faculty matter," announced Mr. Brooke deprecatingly, "and asks to be allowed to come in for a minute."

"A faculty matter? Well, in that case——All right, Mr. Brooke, tell him to come in."

As Amy entered eight pairs of eyes regarded him curiously; nine, in fact, for Mr. Brooke, closing the door softly behind the visitor, gazed at him in questioning disapproval.

"Well, Byrd, what can we do for you?" Mr. Fernald smiled, doubtless with the wish to dispel embarrassment. But he needn't have troubled about that, for Amy didn't look or act in the least embarrassed. "I'm afraid," continued the principal, "that I can't offer you a chair, for we're rather busy just now. What was it you wanted to speak of?"

"I guess it looks pretty cheeky, sir, for me to butt in here," replied Amy, with a smile, "but it's rather important, sir, and—and if anything's to be done about it it'll have to be done tonight."

"Really? Well, it does sound important. Suppose you tell us about it, Byrd."

"Thank you, sir." Amy paused, gathering his words in order. "It's this, Mr. Fernald: when we fellows were put on pro—probation, I mean, it was intended that we should all get the same punishment, wasn't it, sir?"

"Let me see, that was the affair of—— Ah, yes, I recall it. Why, yes, Byrd, naturally it was meant to treat you all alike. What complaint have you?"

"It isn't exactly a complaint, sir. But it's this way. There were nine of us altogether. It was my fault in the first place because I put them up to it. They'd never thought of it if I hadn't." Amy glanced at Mr. Moller. "It was a pretty silly piece of business, sir, and we got what we deserved. But—but none of us meant to—to hurt anyone's feelings, sir. It was just a lark. We didn't think that——"

"We'll allow that, Byrd. Please get down to the purpose of this unusual visit," said Mr. Fernald drily.

"Yes, sir. Well, eight of us it doesn't matter so much about. We aren't football men and being on probation doesn't cut so much—I mean it doesn't matter so much. But Tom Hall's a football man, sir, and it's different for him. This is his last year here and losing his place on the team was hard lines. That's what I'm trying to get at, sir. You meant that we were all to be punished the same, but we weren't. It's just about twice as hard on Tom as it is on the rest of us. You see that, sir, don't you?"

There was a moment of silence and then Mr. Simkins coughed. Or did he chuckle? Amy couldn't tell. But the principal dropped his eyes and tapped his blotter with the tip of the pencil he held. At last:

"That's a novel point of view, Byrd," he said. "There may be something in it. But I must remind you that the Law—and the faculty stands for the Law here—takes no cognisance of conditions existing—hem!" Mr. Fernald glanced doubtfully down the table. "Perhaps it should, though. We'll pass that question for the moment. What is it you suggest, Byrd?"

"Well, sir, the team's in punk shape. It was awful today. It needs Tom, sir; needs him awfully. I don't say that we'll beat Claflin if he should play, Mr. Fernald, but I'm mighty sure we won't if he doesn't. And it seemed to me that maybe you and the other faculty members hadn't thought of how much harder you were giving it to Tom than to the rest of us, and that if you did know, realise it, sir, you'd maybe consider that he'd had about enough and let him off so he might play Saturday. The rest of us haven't any kick coming, sir. It's just Tom. And he doesn't know that I'm here, either. We tried to get him to let us petition faculty, but he wouldn't. He said he was going to take the same punishment as the rest of us."

"Then he doesn't agree with your contention, Byrd?"

"Oh, he sees I'm right, Mr. Fernald, but he—he's obstinate!"

Mr. Fernald smiled, as did most of the others.

"Byrd, I think you ought to take a law course," said the principal. "I might answer you as I started to by pointing out that it is no business of ours whether a punishment is going to hit one fellow harder than another; that just because it might should make that one fellow more careful not to transgress. But you've taken the wind out of my sails by getting me to testify that we intended the punishment to be the same for all. You've put us in a difficult place, Byrd. If we should lift probation in Hall's case it would seem that we had different laws for team members than for boys unconnected with athletics. You've made a very eloquent plea, but I don't just see——" Mr. Fernald hesitated. Then: "Possibly someone has some suggestion," he added, and it seemed to Amy that his gaze rested on Mr. Moller for an instant.

At all events it was the new member of the faculty who spoke. "If I might, sir," he said hesitatingly, "I'd like to make the suggestion that probation be lifted from all. It seems to me that that would—would simplify things, Mr. Fernald."

"Hm. Yes. Possibly. As the target of the extremely vulgar proceeding, Mr. Moller, the suggestion coming from you bears weight. Byrd, you'd better get to your studies. You'll learn our decision in the morning. Your action is commendable, my boy, and we'll take that into consideration also. Good-night."

"Good-night, sir. Good-night, sirs. Thank you."

Amy retired unhurriedly, unembarrassedly, and with dignity, as befitted one who had opened the eyes of Authority to the error of its ways!

The next morning Mr. Fernald announced in chapel that at the request of Mr. Moller, and in consideration of good behaviour, the faculty had voted to lift probation from the following students: Hall——

But just there the applause began and the other eight names were not heard.

CHAPTER XXI
THE DOCTOR TELLS A STORY

TUESDAY, with the return of all first-string players to the line-up and the appearance of Tom Hall once more at right guard, practice went about a hundred per cent better, and those who turned out to watch it went back to the campus considerably encouraged. The showing of the team naturally had an effect on the spirit of the mass meeting that evening. Ever since the Southby game the school had been holding meetings and "getting up steam" for the Claflin contest, but they had been tame affairs in contrast with tonight's. Brimfield was football-crazy now, for the Big Game loomed enormous but four days away. Fellows read football in the papers, talked football and, some of them, dreamed football. The news from Claflin was read and discussed eagerly. The fortunes of the rival eleven were watched just as closely as those of the home team. When a Claflin player wrenched an ankle Brimfield gasped excitedly. When it was published that Cox, of the blue team, had dropped fourteen goals out of twenty tries from the thirty-five-yard line and at a severe angle, depression prevailed at Brimfield. The news that the Claflin scrubs had held the first to only one touchdown in thirty minutes of play sent Brimfield's spirits soaring! Fellows neglected lessons brazenly and during that week of the final battle there was a scholastic slump that would undoubtedly have greatly alarmed the faculty if the latter, rendered wise by experience, hadn't expected it.

The first team players were excused from study hour subsequent to Monday in order that they might attend blackboard lectures and signal drills in the gymnasium. On Tuesday night, after an hour's session, and in response to public clamour, they filed onto the platform just before the meeting was to begin at nine-fifteen and, somewhat embarrassedly, seated themselves in the chairs arranged across the back. Mr. Fernald was there, and Mr. Conklin, the athletic director, and Coaches Robey and Boutelle, and Trainer Danny Moore, and Manager Morton and Childers, captain of the baseball team. And Steve Payne was at the piano. Also, sitting beside Mr. Robey, was Doctor Proctor.

Childers, who was cheer leader that Fall, presided, and, after the assemblage had clapped and shouted "A-a-ay!" as each newcomer appeared on the platform, opened proceedings with the School Song. Then Mr. Fernald spoke briefly, Captain Edwards followed, each being cheered loudly and long, and Childers introduced Mr. Robey. "What we are all anxious to know tonight," said Childers, "is whether we're going to win next Saturday. Mr. Fernald has said that he hopes we shall, Captain Edwards has said that he thinks we shall, and now we're going to hear from the only one who knows! Fellows, a long cheer for Mr. Robey, and make it good! Are you all ready? Now then! One—two—three!"

"Brimfield! Brimfield! Brimfield! Rah, rah, rah! Rah, rah, rah! Rah, rah, rah! Brimfield! Brimfield! Brimfield! Robey!"

When the cheering, and the shouting and clapping and stamping that followed for good measure, had quieted down, Mr. Robey said: "Fellows, Captain Childers is much too flattering. I'm not gifted with second-sight, even if he thinks so. I don't know any more than he does or you do whether we're going to win on Saturday. Like Mr. Fernald, I hope we are and, like Captain Edwards, I think we are." Cheers interrupted then. "But I don't want to make any prediction. I'll say one thing, though, and that is this: If the team plays the way it can play, if it makes full use of the ability that's in it, there's only one thing that can happen, and that's a

114

Brimfield victory! I've got every reason to expect that the team will do its utmost, and that is why I say that I think we'll win. We must remember that we're going up against a strong team, a team that in some ways has shown itself so far this season our superior. I don't say that the Claflin eleven is any better than ours. I don't think so, not for a moment. Our team this Fall is as good as last year's team. We've had our little upsets; we always do; but we've come down to practically the eve of the game in good shape. Every fellow has done his best and, I am firmly convinced, is going to do a little better than his best on Saturday afternoon. And that little better is what will decide the game, fellows. After the coaches have done their part and the players have toiled hard and earnestly and enthusiastically, why then it all comes down to fight! And so it's fight that's going to win the game.

"You fellows must do your part, though. You must be right back of the team, every minute—and let them know it. Cheering helps a team to win, no matter what anyone may say to the contrary. Only cheer at the right times, fellows. Just making a noise indiscriminately is poor stuff. But I don't need to tell you this, I guess, because your cheer leader knows what to do better than I do. But let the team know that you're right with them, backing them up all the time, fighting behind them, boosting them along! It counts, fellows, take my word for it!

"And now there's one other thing I want to say before I make way for someone who can really talk. It's this, fellows. Don't forget the team that has helped us all season, the team that doesn't get into the limelight. And don't forget the coach, who has worked just as hard, perhaps a good deal harder, to develop that team than I've worked. I'm going to ask you to show your appreciation of the unselfish devotion of Coach Boutelle and one of the finest second teams Brimfield has ever had!"

Mr. Robey bowed and retreated and Childers jumped to his feet.

"A cheer for Coach Boutelle, fellows!" he shouted. "A long cheer and a whopper!" And, when it had been given lustily: "And now one for the second team!" he cried. "Everyone into it! One—two—three!" The enthusiasm was mounting high now, and, after the cheer had died away, there were demands for a song. "We want to sing!" proclaimed the meeting. "We want to sing!"

Childers held up a hand. "All right, fellows! Just a minute, please! We've got a guest with us this evening, an honoured guest, fellows. Those of you who know football history know his name as well as you know the names of Heffelfinger and DeWitt and Coy and

Brickley and—and many others in the Football Hall of Fame! I know you want to hear from him and I hope he will be willing to say a few words." Childers glanced at Doctor Proctor and the latter, smiling, shook his head energetically. "He says he will be glad to, fellows," continued Childers mendaciously, amidst laughter, "and so I'm going to call first for a cheer for—if the gentleman will pardon me— 'Gus' Proctor, famous Princeton and All-America tackle, and after that we're going to listen very attentively to him. Now, then, everyone into this! A long cheer for Doctor Proctor!"

"I'm an awfully poor speaker, fellows," began the doctor, when he had advanced to the front of the platform. "I appreciate this honour and if I don't do justice to the fine reputation your—your imaginative cheer leader has provided me with you must try to forgive me. Speaking isn't my line. If any of you would like to have a leg sawed off or something of that sort I'd be glad to do it free of charge just to prove that—well, that there's something I can do fairly decently!

"I saw your team practice yesterday and I thought then that perhaps an operation would benefit it. Then I saw it again today and discovered that my first diagnosis was wrong. Fellows, I call it a good team. I think you've got material there that's equal to any I've ever seen on a school team. Your coach says he won't prophesy as to your game on Saturday. I've known George Robey for ten years. He isn't a bad sort, take him all around, but he's a pessimist of the most pessimistic sort. He's the kind of chap who, if you sprang that old reliable one on him about every cloud having a silver lining, would shrug his shoulders and say, 'Humph! More likely nickel-plated!' That's the sort he is, boys. Now I'm just the opposite, and, at the risk of displeasing George, I'm going to tell you that, from what I've seen of the Brimfield football team in practice, I'm firmly convinced that it's going to win!"

Loud and prolonged cheering greeted that prediction, and it was fully a minute before the speaker could proceed.

"I've played the game in my day and I've coached teams, boys, and I think I've got a little of what your coach disclaimed. I mean a sort of—well, not second-sight, but a sort of ability to tell what a team will do from the looks of the players on it. In my profession we have to study human nature a lot and we get so we can classify folks after we've looked them over and watched them awhile. We make mistakes sometimes, but on the whole we manage fairly well to put folks in the classes they belong in. Doing that with the members of your team I find that almost without exception they class with the kind of fellows who don't like to be beaten! And when a fellow doesn't like to be beaten he isn't—not very often.

"I think I can read in the faces I see here tonight a great deal of that same spirit, and if the team has it and you fellows behind the team have it, why, I wouldn't give a last year's plug-hat for Claflin's chances next Saturday!

"Football," continued Doctor Proctor presently, "is a fine game. It's fun to play and it's a wonderful thing to train a fellow's body and mind. I've heard lots of folks object to it on various scores, but I've never heard an objection yet that carried any weight. More often than not those who run football down don't know the game. Why, if it did no more than teach us obedience and discipline it would be worth while. But it does far more than that. It gives us strong, dependable bodies, it teaches us to think—and think quick, and it gives us courage, physical and moral. I'm going to tell you of an incident that I witnessed only a few weeks since if you'll let me. I fear I'm taking up too much time——"

There were cries of "No, no!" and "Go ahead!"

"I'll try to be brief. Last Fall I was travelling on a train out my way, to be exact some eighty miles west of Cincinnati, when we had an accident. A freight train was slow about taking a side track and we came along and banged into it. It was about five o'clock in the morning and most of the passengers were asleep. A wreck's a nasty thing in any case, but when it happens at night or before it is light enough to see it is worse. The forward cars of our train and the freight caught fire from the engines, and there was a good deal of loose steam around, and things were pretty messy for awhile. There happened to be another doctor on the train and, as soon as we got our bearings, we started a first-aid camp alongside the track. Some of the passengers, mostly in the day coaches up front, were badly burned and we had our hands full.

"There is always more or less confusion in an affair of that sort and it was some minutes after the accident before the rescue work got under way. But one of the first rescuers I noticed was a young chap, a boy in fact, probably about seventeen years old. He didn't have a great deal on, I remember, but he was certainly Johnny-on-the-spot that morning! It was he who brought the first patient to me, a little dried-up Hebrew peddler I judged him, who had been caught under some wreckage in the forward day-coach. He had a broken forearm and while I was busy with him I saw this young chap climbing in and out of windows and wading through wreckage and always coming out again with someone. How many folks he pulled away from the flames and the scalding steam I don't know, but I never saw anyone work harder or more—more efficiently. Yes, efficiently is just the word I want! And I said to myself at the time: 'That fellow is a football man! And I'll bet he's a good one!' You see, it wasn't only that he had courage to risk himself, but he had the ability to see what was to be done and to do it, and do it quick! Why, he was pulling injured women and children and men from those burning, overturned cars before a grown-up man had sensed what had happened! And later on, when we'd done what we could for the burned and scalded bodies and limbs, I got hold of the boy for a moment. I asked him his name and he told it, and then I said: 'You've played football, haven't you?' And he said he had, a little. He wasn't much of a talker, and when some of us said some nice things about what he had done he got horribly fussed and tried to get away. But someone wanted to shake hands with him, and he wouldn't, and I saw that his own hand was burned all inside the palm, deep and nasty. 'How did you do that?' I asked him as I dressed it. Oh, he didn't know. He thought he'd got his hand caught between some beams or something; couldn't get it out for a minute. It wasn't much of a burn! Well, the wrecking train and a hospital train came along about then and I lost sight of that chap, and I didn't see him again.

"I've told the story because I think it bears me out when I say that football is fine training. I don't say that that boy wouldn't have been just as brave and eager to help if he hadn't been a football player, but I do maintain that he wouldn't have known what to do as readily or how to do it and wouldn't have got at it as quickly. And when the flames are eating their way back from car to car quickness means a whole lot! That's the end of my story, boys. But while I've been telling it I've been looking for some sign to tell me that you recognised the hero of it. I don't find the sign and I'm puzzled. Perhaps you're so accustomed to heroes here at Brimfield that one more or less doesn't stir you. For the satisfaction of my own curiosity I'm going to ask you if you know who I've been talking about."

A deep silence was the only answer. The doctor's audience looked extremely interested and curious, but no one spoke.

"I see. You don't know. Well, perhaps I'd better not tell then." But a chorus of protest arose. The doctor hesitated, and his gaze seemed to rest intently on a spot at one side of the hall and about half-way back. Finally, when silence had fallen again: "I guess I will tell," he said. "It can't do him or you any harm. It may help a little to know that there's one amongst you fine enough to do what I've described. I've never seen that boy from the moment the wrecking

118

train reached the scene of the wreck until tonight, and so I've never spoken to him again. But as I sat on the platform here awhile ago I looked and saw him. I don't forget faces very easily, and as you can understand, I wasn't likely to forget his. As I say, I haven't spoken to him yet, but I'm going to now."

There was a silence in which a dropped pin would have made a noise like a crowbar. Half the audience had turned their heads in the direction of Doctor Proctor's smiling gaze, but all eyes were fixed on his lips. The breathless silence lengthened. Then the doctor spoke.

"How is your hand, Gilbert?" he asked.

CHAPTER XXII
COACH ROBEY IS PUZZLED

SOME twenty minutes later Don dropped into a chair in Number 6 and heaved a deep sigh of relief. "Gee," he muttered, "I wouldn't go through that again for—for a million dollars!"

Tim chuckled as he seated himself beyond the table. "Why not?" he asked innocently. "I thought everyone treated you very nicely."

A smile flitted across Don's face. "I suppose they did, only—I guess that was the trouble! I felt like an awful fool, Tim! Look here, what did he have to go and tell everything he knew for? I was afraid he was going to and I wanted like anything to sneak out of there, but the place was so quiet I didn't have the nerve! At first I didn't suspect that he had seen me. I didn't recognise him until he stood up to speak this evening. Yesterday I thought he looked sort of familiar, but I couldn't place him. He—he talks too much!"

"He said some awfully nice things about you, old man."

"He said a lot of nonsense, too! Exaggerated the whole thing, he did. Why, to listen to him you'd think I saved about a thousand people from certain death! Well, I didn't. I helped about six or seven folks out of those cars. They were sort of rattled and didn't seem to know enough to beat it."

"They weren't in any danger, then?"

"No, not much. All they had to do was crawl out of the way."

"Then they weren't any of them burned, Don?"

"A few were."

"How about the man with the broken arm?"

"Oh, he'd got caught somehow." Don looked up and saw Tim's laugh. "Well," he added defensively, "he needn't have told about it like that, right out in front of the whole school, need he?"

"You bet he need! Donald, you're a bloomin', blushin' hero, and we're proud of you! And when I say blushing I mean it, for you haven't stopped yet!"

"I guess you'd blush," growled Don, "if it happened to you!"

"I dare say, but it never will. I'll never have the whole school get up on their feet and cheer me like mad for three solid minutes! And I'll never have Josh shake my hand off and beam at me and tell me I'm a credit to the school! Such beautiful things are not for poor little Tim!"

Don sighed. "Well, it's over with, anyway."

"Over with, nothing! It won't be over with as long as you stay here, Donald. A hero you are and a hero you remain, old chap. And—and I'm mighty proud of you, you old humbug! Telling us you didn't do anything but help lug folks to the relief train, or something!"

"I didn't say that," replied Don defensively.

"You let us think it. Gee, if I'd done anything like that I'd have put it in the papers!" Tim chuckled and then went on seriously. "You don't need to worry about the fellows thinking you a quitter any more, do you? I guess Proctor settled that once and for all, Don. And suppose you'd run away home the other night. This wouldn't have happened and fellows would have said you had a yellow streak. I guess it was a mighty lucky thing you have little Tim to look after you, dearie!"

"I'm glad I didn't," said Don earnestly. "I'd have made a worse mess of it, shouldn't I? I—I'm sorry you got that punch, though, Timmy."

"Forget it! It was worth it! Being the room-mate of a hero atones for everything you ever did to me, Donald. I'm that proud——"

But Tim didn't finish, for Don started around the table for him.

* * *

At the time this conversation was taking place Mr. Robey and Doctor Proctor were walking back to the former's room in the village through a frosty, starlit night.

"You certainly managed to spring a sensation, Gus," observed the coach as they turned into the road.

"I should say so! Well, that boy deserved all the cheering and praise he received. And I'm glad I told that story."

"Well, it's got me guessing," responded the other. "Look here, Gus, take a chap like the one you described tonight. What would you think if he quit cold a week before the big game?"

"Quit? How do you mean, George?"

"Just that. Develops an imaginary illness. Tells you he doesn't feel well enough to play, in spite of the fact that he has nothing more the matter with him than you or I have. Probably not so much. Shows absolute relief when you tell him he's dropped. What would you say to that?"

"You mean Gilbert did that?" Mr. Robey assented. "I wondered why he wasn't on the platform with the rest of the team," mused the doctor. "I'd say there was something queer about it, George. When did this happen?"

"Last week. Thursday or Friday, I think. He'd been laid off for a day or so and I thought he'd gone a bit fine, although he's rather too phlegmatic to suffer much from nerves. Some of the high-strung chaps do go to pieces about this time and you have to nurse them along pretty carefully. But Gilbert! Well, on Saturday—yes, that was the day—he'd been reported perfectly fit by the trainer and just as a matter of form I asked him if he was ready to play. And, by Jove, he had the cheek to face me and say he wasn't well enough! It was nonsense, of course. He'd simply got scared. I told him so and dropped him. But it's curious that a boy who could do what you told of this evening could prove a quitter like that."

"You say he seemed relieved when you let him go?"

"Yes, he showed it plainly."

"That is funny! I wonder what the truth of it is?"

"Nerves, I suppose. Cold feet, as the fellows say."

"Never! There's something else, old man, that you haven't got hold of. Can he play?"

"Y-yes. Yes, he can play. He's the sort that comes slow and plays a bit logy, but he's steady and works hard. Not a brilliant man, you know, but dependable. He's been playing guard. Losing him has left us a bit weak on that side, too."

"Why not take him back then? Look here, George, you're a good coach and all that, but you're a mighty poor judge of human nature."

"Piffle!"

"It's so, though. You've only got to study that chap Gilbert to see that he isn't the quitting kind. His looks show it, his manner shows it, the way he talks shows it. He's the sort that might want to

121

quit; we all do sometimes; but he couldn't because he's got stuff in him that wouldn't let him!"

"That's all well enough, Gus, but facts are facts. Gilbert did quit, and quit cold on me. So theories don't count for much. And this human nature flapdoodle——"

"I don't say he didn't quit. But I do say that you've made the wrong diagnosis, George. Did you talk to him? Ask him what the trouble was? Go after the symptoms?"

"No, I'm no physician. He said he wasn't feeling well enough to play. I told him we had no place for quitters on the team. He had nothing to say to that. If you think I can feel the pulse and look at the tongue of every fellow——"

Doctor Proctor laughed. "And take his temperature too, eh? No, I don't expect you to do that, George. But I'll tell you what I would do, and I'd do it tomorrow too. I'd call around and see Gilbert. I'd tell him that I wasn't satisfied with the explanation he'd made and I'd ask him to make a clean breast of the trouble, for he must be in some trouble or he wouldn't thank you for firing him. And then I'd stop cutting off my nose to spite my face and I'd reinstate him tomorrow afternoon!"

"Hmph! The trouble with you doctors is that you're too romantic. You imagine things, you——"

"We have to imagine, George. If we stuck to facts we'd never get anywhere in our profession! You try a little imagination, old chap. You're too matter-of-fact. What you can't see you won't believe in."

"I certainly won't! As the kids say, seeing's believing."

"Well, there's a very unattractive board fence across the road, George. On the other side of it there are shrubs and grass. I can't see them, but I know they're there."

"More likely tin-cans and ashes," grunted Mr. Robey.

"Pessimist!" laughed the other. "But never mind; ashes or grass, something's there, and you can't see it and yet you've got to acknowledge the existence of it. Now haven't you?"

"I suppose so, but"—Mr. Robey laughed—"I'd rather see it!"

"Climb the fence and have a look then! But you'll try my plan with the boy, won't you?"

"Yes, I will. If only to satisfy my curiosity, Gus. Hang it, the chap can't be a quitter!"

"He isn't. I'll stake my reputation as—as a romanticist on that! I'd like mighty well to stay and solve the mystery with you, but I'll have to jump for that early train. I wish, though, that you'd drop me a line and tell me the outcome. I'm interested—and puzzled."

"All right. I'm not much of a letter-writer, though. I'll see you before you go back and tell you about it. You'll be in New York on Sunday, won't you?"

"Until two o'clock. Have lunch with me and see me off. Come to the hotel as early as you can and we'll hold post-mortems on the games. Let's hope that Princeton and Brimfield both win next Saturday, George!"

CHAPTER XXIII
CROSS-EXAMINATION

DON found being a hero an embarrassing business the next day. The masters bothered him by stopping and shaking hands and saying nice things, and the fellows beamed on him if they weren't well enough acquainted to speak and insisted on having a full and detailed history of that train-wreck if they were! Of course they all, masters and students, meant well and wanted to show their admiration, but Don wished they wouldn't. It made him feel horribly self-conscious, and feeling self-conscious was distinctly uncomfortable. At breakfast table his companions referred to last evening's incident laughingly and poked fun at Don and enjoyed his embarrassment, but it wasn't difficult to tell that Doctor Proctor's narrative had made a strong impression on them and increased their liking for Don. When, just before Don had finished his meal, Mr. Robey left the training-table and crossed the room toward him he braced himself for another scene in which he would have to stand up and be shaken by the hand, and possibly, and worst of all, listen to some sort of an apology from the coach. But Don was spared, for Mr. Robey only placed a hand on the back of his chair, included the rest of the occupants of the table in his "Good-morning," and said carelessly: "Gilbert, I wish you'd drop over to Mr. Conklin's office some time this morning and see me. What time can you come?"

"Half-past ten, sir?"

"That will be all right, thanks."

The coach returned to his table, leaving Don wondering what was up. Possibly, he thought, the coach wanted to make some sort of retraction of his accusation of Saturday, although Don didn't believe that Mr. Robey was the sort to funk a public apology. If it wasn't that it could only be that he was to be offered his place on the team again. Don sighed. That would be beastly, for he would have to tell more fibs, and brand new ones, too, since not even a blind man would believe him ill now! It was something of a coincidence that Don should run across Walton in the corridor a few minutes later. Don was for passing by with no recognition of the other, but Walton, with a smirk, placed himself fairly in the way.

"Great stuff, Gilbert," he said with an attempted heartiness. "Some hero, eh, what?"

"Drop it, Walton!" Don lowered his voice, for others were passing toward the doorway. "And I'll thank you not to speak to me. You know my opinion of you. Now shut up!"

Walton found nothing to say until it was too late. Don approached the gymnasium after his ten o'clock recitation with lagging feet. He had scant taste for the impending interview and would have gladly avoided it if such a thing had been possible. But he didn't see any way out of it and he heard the big door bang to behind him with a sinking heart. Why, he hadn't even thought up any new excuse!

Mr. Robey and Mr. Conklin, the athletic director, were both in the latter's room when Don knocked at the half-opened door. Mr. Conklin said "Good-morning" and then followed it with: "I've got something to attend to on the floor, Robey, if you'll excuse me," and went out, closing the door behind him. Don wished he had stayed. He took the chair vacated by the director and faced Coach Robey with as much ease as he could assume, which was very little. The coach began without much preamble.

"I didn't ask you over here to talk about last night, Gilbert, or to offer you any apology for what I said on the field last Saturday. I don't believe much in spoken apologies. If I'm wrong I show it and there's no mistake about it. I think I was wrong in your case, Gilbert. And I'll say so, if you like, very gladly, and act so if you'll prove it."

"I don't want any apology, sir," answered Don. "I guess you were right enough."

"Well, that's what I want to find out. What was the trouble, Gilbert?"

"Why, just what I said, Coach. I—I didn't feel very fit and I didn't think it would be any use playing, feeling like I did. If you don't feel well you can't play very well, and so I thought I'd say so. I didn't mind being dropped, sir. I deserved it. And—and that's quite all right." Don got up, his eyes shifting to the door.

"Wait a minute! Let's get the truth of this. You're lying, aren't you?"

Don tried to look indignant and failed, tried to look hurt and failed again. Then he gave it up and dropped his gaze before the searching eyes of the other. "I'm feeling some better now," he muttered.

Coach Robey laughed shortly. "Gilbert, you can't lie worth a cent! Now, look here. I'm your friend. Why not come across and tell me what's up? I know you weren't sick. Danny gave you a clean bill of health that morning. And I know you haven't got any nerves to speak of. There's something else, Gilbert. Now what is it?"

"Nothing, sir."

"Then why did you act that way?"

"I—I just didn't want to play."

"Didn't want to play! Why not?"

"I wasn't doing very well, and it was pretty hard work, and there was Walton after the place, too. He could play better than I could."

"Who told you so? Walton?" asked the coach drily.

"I could see it," murmured Don.

"So you were suddenly afraid of hard work, eh? It had never bothered you before, had it? Last year or this year either?"

"No, I guess not."

"Perhaps it was more because you felt that Walton would be a better man for the place, then?" surmised the coach.

Don agreed eagerly. It was a case of any port in a storm by now and he was glad enough to have the coach find an explanation. "Yes, sir, I guess that was it."

"Well, that was generous of you," said the other approvingly. "But didn't it occur to you that perhaps I would be a better one to decide that matter than you? You've never known me to keep a fellow on the team for sentimental reasons, have you?"

"No, sir."

"Hm. Now when was it—I mean how long before last Saturday was it—that you and Walton talked it over?"

"Sir?" Don looked up startledly. "I—we—there wasn't any talk about it," he stammered.

"Well, what did Walton say?"

Don hesitated, studying Mr. Robey's face in the hope of discovering how much that gentleman knew. Finally: "When do you mean?" he asked.

"I mean the time you and Walton talked about which was the best man for the position," replied the other easily. To himself he reflected that he was following Gus Proctor's advice with a vengeance! But he was by this time pretty certain of his ground.

"I don't remember that we ever—exactly did that," Don faltered. "There was some talk, maybe, but he—he never said anything like that."

"Like what?"

"Why, that he was a better guard."

"Then what put the idea in your head, Gilbert?"

"I suppose I just saw it myself."

"But you were playing the position pretty regularly before Thursday or whatever day it was you were taken ill, weren't you?"

"Yes, sir."

"Then how could you tell that Walton was better?"

"I don't know. He—he seemed better. And then Tim told me I was too slow."

"Tim Otis? Otis had better mind his own business," grumbled the coach. "So that was it, then. All right. I'm glad to get the truth of the matter." The little tightening of Don's mouth didn't escape him. "Now, then, I'm going to surprise you, Gilbert. I'm going to surprise you mightily. I'm going to tell you that Walton is not a better left guard than you. He isn't nearly so good. That does surprise you, doesn't it?"

Don nodded, his eyes fixed uneasily on the coach's.

"Well, there it is, anyway. And so I think the best thing for all of us, Gilbert, is for you to come back to work this afternoon."

Don's look of dismay quite startled the other.

"But I'd rather not, sir! I—I'm out of practice now. I've quit training. I've been eating all sorts of things; potatoes and fresh bread and pastry—no end of pastry, sir!—and—and candy——"

Mr. Robey grunted. "You don't show it," he said. "Anyway, I guess that won't matter. I'll chance it. Three o'clock, then, Gilbert."

Don's gaze sought the floor and he shook his head. "I'd rather not, sir, if you don't mind," he muttered.

"But I do mind. The team needs you, Gilbert! And now that I know that you didn't quit because you were afraid——"

"I did, though!" Don looked up desperately. "That was the truth of it!"

Mr. Robey sighed deeply. "Gilbert," he said patiently, "if I couldn't lie better than you can I wouldn't try it! You weren't afraid and you aren't afraid and you know it and I know it! So, then, is it Walton?"

After a moment Don nodded silently.

"You think he's a better man than you are, eh?"

Don nodded again, but hesitatingly.

126

"Or you've taken pity on him and want him to play against Claflin, perhaps."

"Yes, sir. You see, his folks are going to be here and they'll expect him to play!"

"Oh, I see. You and Walton come from the same town? But of course you don't. How did you know his folks were coming, then?"

"He told me."

"When?"

"About—some time last week."

"Was it the day you had that talk about the position and which of you was to have it?"

"I guess so. Yes, sir, it was that time."

"And he, perhaps, suggested that it would be a nice idea for you to back out and let him in, eh?"

Don was silent.

"Did he?" insisted the coach.

"He said that his folks were coming——"

"And that he'd like to get into the game so they wouldn't be disappointed?"

"Something like that," murmured Don.

"And you consented?"

"Not exactly, but I thought it over and—and——"

Mr. Robey suddenly leaned forward and laid a hand on Don's knee.

"Gilbert," he asked quietly, "what has Walton got on you?"

CHAPTER XXIV
"ALL READY, BRIMFIELD?"

THOSE who braved a chill east wind and went out that afternoon to watch practice enjoyed a sensation, for when the first team came trotting over from the gymnasium, a half-hour later because of a rigorous signal quiz, amongst them, dressed to play, was Don Gilbert! A buzz of surprise and conjecture travelled through the ranks of the shivering onlookers, that speedily gave place to satisfaction, and as Don, tossing aside his blanket, followed the first-string players into the field a small and enthusiastic First Form youth clapped approvingly, others took it up and in a moment the applause crackled along the side line.

"That's for you," whispered Tim to Don. "Lift off your head-guard!"

But Don glanced alarmedly toward the fringe of spectators and hid as best he could behind Thursby! Practice went with a new vim today. Doubtless the return of Don heartened the team, for one thing, and then there was a snap of winter in the air that urged to action. The second was as nearly torn to tatters this afternoon as it had ever been, and the first scored twice in each of the two fifteen-minute periods. "Boutelle's Babies" were a lame and tired aggregation when the final whistle blew!

Later it became known that Walton was out of it, had emptied his locker and retired from football affairs for the year. All sorts of stories circulated. One had it that he had quarrelled with Coach Robey and been incontinently "fired." Another that he had become huffy over Gilbert's reinstatement and had resigned. None save Don and Coach Robey and Walton himself knew the truth of the matter for a long time. Don did tell Tim eventually, but that was two years later, when his vow of secrecy had lapsed. Just now he was about as communicative as a sphinx, and Tim's eager curiosity had to go unsatisfied.

"But what did he say?" Tim demanded after practice that afternoon. "He must have said something!"

Don considered leisurely. "No, nothing special. He said I was to report for work."

"Well, what did you say?"

"I said I would!"

"Well, what about Walton? Where does he get off?"

"I don't know."

Tim gestured despairingly. "Gee, you're certainly a chatty party! Don't tell me any more, please! You may say something you'll be sorry for!"

"I'll tell you some day all about it, Tim. I can't now. I said I wouldn't."

"Then there is something to tell, eh? I knew it! You can't fool your Uncle Dudley like that, Donald! Tell me just one thing and I'll shut up. Did you and Walton have a row the time you went to see him in his room?"

Don shook his head. "No, we didn't."

"Well, then, why——"

"You said you'd shut up," reminded the other.

"Oh, all right," grumbled Tim. "Anyway, I'm mighty glad. Every fellow on the team is as pleased as Punch. I guess the whole

128

school is, too. It was mighty decent of Robey, wasn't it? Do you know, Don, Robey's got a lot of sense for a football coach?"

Don often wondered what had occurred and been said at the interview between Mr. Robey and Harry Walton. The coach had sworn Don to silence at the termination of their interview. "If Walton asks you whether you told me about the business you can say you did, if you like. Or tell him I wormed it out of you, which is just about what I did do. But don't say anything to anyone else about it; at all events, not as long as Walton's here. I'm going to find him now and have a talk with him. I don't think you need be at all afraid of anything he may do after I get through with him. You fellows clearly did wrong in outstaying leave that night, but you had a fairly good excuse and if you'd had enough sense to go to faculty the next morning and explain you'd have all got off with only a lecture, I guess. Your mistake was in not confessing. However, I don't consider it my place to say anything. It's an old story now, anyhow. Be at the gym at three with your togs, Gilbert, and do your best for us from now on. I'm glad to have you back again. What I said that afternoon you'd better forget. I'll show the school that I've changed my mind about you. I suppose I ought to make some sort of an apology, but——"

"Please don't say anything more about it, sir," begged Don.

"Well, I'll say this, Gilbert: You acted like a white man in taking your medicine and keeping the others out of trouble. You certainly deserve credit for that."

"I don't see it," replied the boy. "I don't see what else I could have done, Mr. Robey!"

The coach pondered a moment. Then he laughed. "I guess you're right, at that! Just the same, you did what was square, Gilbert. All right, then. Three o'clock." He held out his hand and Don put his in it, and the two gripped firmly.

Hurrying back to Main Hall, Don regretted only one thing, which was that he had in a way broken his agreement with Walton to say nothing about their bargain. Coach Robey, though, had pointed out that the agreement had been terminable by either party to it, and that in confessing to him Don had been within his rights. "Walton can now go ahead and take the matter to faculty, as he threatened to do," said the coach. "Only, when I get through talking to him I don't think he will care to!"

And apparently he hadn't, for no dire summons reached Don from the office that day or the next, nor did he ever hear more of the matter. Walton displayed a retiring disposition that was new and novel. On such infrequent occasions as Don ran across him Walton

129

failed to see him. The day of the game the latter was in evidence with his father, mother and younger brother; Don saw him making the rounds of the buildings with them and he wondered in what manner Walton had accounted to his folks for his absence from the football team. Walton stayed on at school, very little in evidence, until Christmas vacation, but when the fellows reassembled after the recess he was not amongst them. Rumour had it that he had been taken ill and would not be back. Rumour was proved partly right, at all events, for Brimfield knew him no more.

* * *

The first and second teams held final practice on Thursday. The first only ran through signals for awhile, did some punting and catching and then disappeared, leaving the second to play two fifteen-minute periods with a team composed of their own second-string and the first team's third-string players. After that was over, the second winning without much effort, the audience, which had cheered and sung for the better part of an hour, marched back to the gymnasium and did it some more, and the second team, cheering most enthusiastically for themselves and the first and the school and, last but by no means least, for Mr. Boutelle, joyously disbanded for the season.

There was another mass-meeting that evening, an intensely fervid one, followed by a parade about the campus and a good deal of noise that was finally quelled by Mr. Fernald when, in response to demands, he appeared on the porch of the Cottage and made a five-minute speech which ended with the excellent advice to return to hall and go to bed.

The players didn't attend the meeting that night, nor were they on hand at the one that took place the night following. Instead, they trotted and slithered around the gymnasium floor in rubber-soled shoes and went through their entire repertoire of plays under the sharp eyes of Coaches Robey and Boutelle. There was a blackboard lecture, too, on each evening, and when, at nine-thirty on Friday, they were dismissed, with practice all over for the year, most of them were very glad to slide into bed as quickly as possible. If any of them had "the jumps" that night it was after they were asleep, for the coach had tired them out sufficiently to make them forget that such things as nerves were a part of their system!

But the next morning was a different matter. Those who had never gone through a Claflin contest were inclined to be finicky of appetite and to go off into trances with a piece of toast or a fork-full of potato poised between plate and mouth. Even the more experienced fellows showed some indication of strain. Thursby, for instance, who had been three years on the first team as substitute or first-choice centre, who had already taken some part in two Claflin games, and who was apparently far too big and calm to be affected by nerves, showed a disposition to talk more than was natural.

Don never really remembered at all clearly how that Saturday morning passed. Afterward he had vague recollections of sitting in Clint Thayer's room and hearing Amy Byrd rattle off a great deal of nonsensical advice to him and Clint and Tim as to how to conduct themselves before the sacrifice (Amy had insisted that they should line up and face the grand-stand before the game commenced, salute and recite the immortal line of Claudius's gladiators: "Morituri te salutant!"); of seeing Manager Jim Morton dashing about hither and thither, scowling blackly under the weight of his duties; of wandering across to the woods beyond the baseball field with Tim Otis and Larry Jones and some others and sitting on the stone wall there and watching Larry take acorns out of Tim's ears and nose; and, finally, of going through a perfectly farcical early dinner in a dining hall empty save for the members of the training-table. After that events stood out more clearly in his memory.

Claflin's hosts began to appear at about half-past one. They wore blue neckties and arm-bands or carried blue pennants which they had the good taste to keep furled while they wandered around the campus and poked inquisitive heads into the buildings. Then the Claflin team, twenty-six strong, rolled up in two barges just before two, having taken their dinner at the village inn, disembarked in front of Wendell and meandered around to the gymnasium laden with suit-cases and things looking insultingly care-free and happy, and, as it couldn't be denied, particularly husky!

Don, observing from the steps of Torrence, wondered how they managed to appear so easy and careless. No one, as he confided to Tom Hall and Tim, would ever suspect that they were about to do battle for the Brimfield-Claflin championship!

"Huh," said Tom, "that's nothing. That's the way we all do when we go away to play. It's this sticking at home and having nothing to do but think that takes the starch out of you. When you go off you feel as if you were on a lark. Things take your mind off your troubles. But, just the same, a lot of those grinning dubs are doing a heap of worrying about now. They aren't nearly as happy as they look!"

"They're a lot happier than they're going to be about three hours from now," said Tim darkly. That struck the right note, and

131

Tom and Don laughed, and Tim laughed with them, and they all three put their shoulders back and perked up a lot!

And then it was two o'clock and they were pulling on their togs in the locker-room; and Danny Moore was circulating about in very high spirits, cracking jokes and making them laugh, and Coach Robey was dispatching Jim Morton and Jim's assistant on mysterious errands and referring every little while to his red-covered memorandum book and looking very untroubled and serene. And then there was a clamping of feet on the stairs above and past the windows some two dozen pairs of blue-stockinged legs moved briskly as the visitors went across to the field for practice. And suddenly the noise was stilled and Coach Robey was telling them that it was up to them now, and that they hadn't a thing in the world to do for the next two hours but knock the tar out of those blue-clad fellows, and that they had a fine day for it! And then, laughing hard and cheering a little, they piled out and across the warm, sunlit grass, past the line of fellow-students and home-folks and towners, with here and there a pretty girl to glance shyly and admiringly at them as they trotted by, and so to the bench. Nerves were gone now. They were only eager and impatient. "Squads out!" sang Mr. Robey. Off came sweaters and faded blankets and they were out on the gridiron, with Carmine and McPhee cheerily piping the signals, with their canvas legs rasping together as they trotted about, and with the Brimfield cheer sounding in their ears, making them feel a little chokey, perhaps, but wonderfully strong and determined and proud!

And presently they were back in front of the bench, laughing at and pummelling one another, and the rival captains and the referee were watching a silver coin turn over and over in the sunlight out there by the tee in midfield. Behind them the stand was packed and colourful. Beyond, Brimfield was cheering lustily again. Across the faded green, at the end of the newly-brushed white lines, nearly a hundred Claflin youths were waving their banners and cheering back confidently.

"Claflin kicks off," sang Captain Edwards. "We take the west goal. Come on, fellows! Everyone on the jump now!"

A long-legged Claflin guard piled the dirt up into a six-inch cone, laid the ball tenderly upon it, viewed the result, altered it, backed off and waited.

"All ready, Claflin? All ready, Brimfield?"

The whistle blew.

CHAPTER XXV
TIM GOES OVER

COACH ROBEY put his best foot forward when the first period started by presenting the strongest line-up he had. Fortunately, Brimfield had reached the Claflin game with every first-string man in top shape, something that doesn't often happen with a team. There was Captain Edwards at left end, Thayer at left tackle, Gilbert at left guard, Thursby at centre, Hall at right guard, Crewe at right tackle, Holt at right end, Carmine at quarter, St. Clair at left half, Otis at right half and Rollins at full.

Opposed to them was a team fully their equal in age, weight and experience. The Claflin forwards were a bit taller and rangier, and their centre, unlike Thursby, was below rather than above average size. Behind their line, the four players were, with the exception of Grady, full-back, small and light. But they were known to be fast and heady and Claflin didn't make the mistake of underestimating their ability. The left half, Cox, was a broken-field runner of renown as well as Claflin's best goal-kicker. Perhaps it would have been difficult that fall to have picked two teams to oppose each other that were more evenly matched than those representing the Maroon-and-Grey and the Blue.

For the first few minutes of play each eleven seemed to be feeling out its opponent. Two exchanges of punts gained ground for neither side. Brimfield got her backfield working then on her twenty yards and St. Clair and Tim tried each side of the blue line and in two downs gained a scant six yards. Rollins punted out at Claflin's forty-seven. The Blue got past Hall for two and slid off Holt for three more. The next rush failed and Claflin punted to Carmine on the fifteen. The Blue's ends were down on Carmine and he was stopped for a five-yard gain. Rollins tried a forward pass to Edwards, but threw short and the ball grounded. Tim Otis ran the left end for four and, on a delayed pass, Rollins heaved himself through centre for the distance, and Brimfield cheered loudly when the linesmen pulled up stakes and trailed the chain ten yards nearer the centre of the field.

A second forward pass was caught by Holt, but he was brought down for a scant three-yard gain. Once more Rollins attempted the centre of the blue line, but this time he was stopped short. On third down Rollins punted and Claflin caught on her forty and ran the ball back to the middle of the field. Claflin then found

Crewe for four yards and completed her distance on a straight plunge between Gilbert and Thayer. It was the Blue's turn to cheer then and she performed valiantly. Claflin tried Edwards's end, but made nothing of it, poked Cox past Crewe for a couple of yards, made three around Holt and then punted. St. Clair misjudged the distance and the ball went over his head and there was a scamper to the goal line. Carmine finally fell on the ball for a touchback and the excitement in the stands subsided. Brimfield smashed Otis at the Blue's centre and reached the twenty-five-yard line. St. Clair made three on a skin-tackle play at the right and Rollins got the distance on a plunge after a fake-kick. Brimfield again made first down on the forty-two yards and her supporters howled gleefully. A moment later they had new cause for rejoicing when Rollins pegged the ball across the field to Edwards and the Maroon-and-Grey's captain scampered and dodged along the side of the field for thirteen yards before he was tackled. Time was called for a Claflin back and Brimfield drew off for a consultation, the result of which was seen in the next play.

Carmine called Gilbert to the right side of centre, the backs spread themselves in wide formation ten yards behind the line and Steve Edwards, as the first signal began, ran back, straightened out as the ball was snapped, raced along behind his forwards and swept around his right end. Claflin's right end and half-back plunged outside of Thayer, were met by St. Clair and Rollins, and Carmine, having taken the ball on a long pass from Thursby, raced past them and then swung quickly in and found an almost clear field ahead.

Two white lines passed under his twinkling feet and then, near the twenty, he was challenged by a Claflin back. Carmine eluded him, crossed a third line, found himself confronted by the Blue's quarter, attempted to slip by on the outside, was tackled and borne struggling across the side line and deposited forcibly on the ground.

When the ball was stepped in by the referee it was set down some four inches inside the fifteen-yard line. In the stands and along the side of the field Brimfield was cheering triumphantly, imploringly, and waving her banners. The linesmen scampered in obedience to the referee's waving arm.

"First down!" shouted the official. "All right, Brimfield? Ready, Claflin?" The whistle piped again.

Rollins was stopped squarely on a try at right guard and Otis made a scant three past the left tackle. Under the shadow of her goal-posts, Claflin was digging her cleats in the turf and fighting hard. Rollins went back. "Get through, Claflin! Block this kick!"

cried the Blue's quarter-back. "Get through! Get through!" Back went the ball from Thursby, a trifle high but straight enough, Rollins poised it, swung his leg, and then, tucking the pigskin under his arm, sprang away to the left. Shouts of alarm, cries of warning, the hurried rush of feet and rasping of canvas! Bodies crashed together and went down. Rollins, at the ten yards now, side-stepped and got past a blue-legged defender, turned in and went banging straight into the mêlée. Arms clutched at him. He was stopped momentarily. Then he wrested free, plunged on for another yard and went to earth.

"Second down!" cried the referee when he had bored through the pile of squirming bodies and found the ball. He glanced along the five-yard line, set the pigskin to earth again, and "About two feet to go!" he added. Brimfield was shouting incessantly now, standing and waving. "Touchdown! Touchdown! Touchdown!" Across the field Claflin sent back a dogged chant: "Hold 'em, Claflin! Hold 'em, Claflin! Hold 'em, Claflin!"

But surely Claflin couldn't do that! It seemed too much to ask or expect. Otis made it first down off left tackle, placing the ball on the three yards. Before the next play could be started the period ended and the teams flocked to the water pails and then tramped down to the other end of the field. The cheering never paused, even if the playing did. Childers, red-faced and perspiring, kept the Brimfield section busy every instant. "Once more, now! A long cheer with nine 'Brimfields'! That's good! Keep it up! We're going to score, fellows! Let's have it again! All into it!"

Only three yards to go and four downs to do it! Claflin lined up desperately, her forwards digging their toes barely inside their last line, her backfield men skirmishing anxiously about behind it. "Push 'em back, Claflin! You can do it! Don't give 'em an inch! Stop 'em right here, fellows! Low, low, get low, you fellows! Charge into 'em and smother this play!" The Claflin quarter, pale of face, thumped crouching backs and watched the foe intently.

"Put it over now!" shrilled Carmine. "Here we go! Get down there, Hall! Signals!"

Rollins leaped forward, took the ball from Carmine and smashed straight ahead. There was a moment of doubt. His plunging body stopped, went on, stopped, was borne back.

"Second down! Two and a half to go!"

Again the signals, the line shifted, Claflin changed to meet the shift. St. Clair slewed across and slammed past the Claflin left tackle. But the secondary defence had him in the next instant and he was thrust, fighting, back and still back. But he had gained. "A yard and a half!" proclaimed the referee.

"You've got to do it, Brimfield!" shouted Edwards intensely. "Don't let them get the jump on you like that! Get into it, Crewe! Watch that man, Gilbert! Come on now! Put it over!"

"Signals!" shrieked Carmine. "Make it go this time! Over with it!"

Back went Rollins, hands outstretched. "Fake!" shouted Claflin. "Watch the ball! Watch the ball!"

Rollins's arms fell, empty, as St. Clair grabbed the pigskin and swept wide to the right. "In! In!" cried Carmine. St. Clair turned and shot toward the broken line. His interference did its part, but the Claflin left end had fooled Holt and it was that blue-legged youth who got St. Clair and thumped him to the sod. An anxious, breathless moment followed. Brimfield called for time and St. Clair, on his back, kicked and squirmed while they pumped the air back into his lungs. The referee, kneeling over the ball, squinted along the line. Then:

"Fourth down and about two to go!" he announced.

St. Clair had lost a half-yard! Claflin cheered weakly. Steve Edwards and Carmine consulted.

"We'd better kick it over," said Carmine. "They're getting the jump on us every time, Steve." Carmine's voice was husky and he had to gasp his words out. Steve, panting like an engine, shook his head.

"We need the touchdown," he said. "We'll put it over. Try 11. Tim can make it."

St. Clair walked back to his place. The whistle sounded again. "Come on, Brimfield!" gasped Carmine. "This is your last chance! If you don't do it this time you'll never do it! Play like you meant it! Stop your fooling and show 'em football! Every man into this and make it go! Hall over! Signals!" Hall pushed his way to the left of the line. Claflin shuffled to meet the change. "Signals! 83—38—11—106!"

"Signals!" cried St. Clair. Carmine turned on him, snarling. "Use your bean! Change signals! Hall over! 61—16—11—37! 61—16—11——"

Back shot the ball to the quarter. Off sped St. Clair around his end, followed by Rollins. Carmine crouched, back to the line, while he counted five. Then Tim Otis shot forward, took the delayed pass, jammed the ball against his stomach and went in past Thursby on the right.

Tim struck the line as if shot out of a gun. There was no hole

136

there, but Tim made one. If the secondary defence, overanxious, had not been fooled by that fake attack at their end Tim would never have gained a foot. But as it was Claflin was caught napping in the centre of her line. Tim banged against a brawny guard, Carmine, following him through, added impetus, the Claflin line buckled inward! Shouts and grunts, stifled groans of despair from the yielding blue line! Then Brimfield closed in behind Tim and he was borne off his feet and on and over to fall at last in a chaos of struggling bodies well across the goal line!

The ball went over to the right of the goal and Carmine decided on a punt-out. Unfortunately, Thayer juggled the catch and so Brimfield lost her try-at-goal. But six points looked pretty big just then and continued to look big all the rest of the half and during the succeeding intermission. Brimfield's supporters were confident and happy. They sang and cheered and laughed, and the sun, sinking behind the wooded ridge, cast long golden beams on the flaunting maroon banners.

And then the teams came trotting back once more and cheers thundered forth from opposing stands. Howard had taken St. Clair's place, it was seen, and Claflin had replaced her right guard. But otherwise the teams were unchanged. Brimfield kicked off and Claflin brought her supporters to their feet by running the ball back all the way to the forty-five-yard line. That was Cox, the fleet-footed and elusive, and the Blue's left half got a mighty cheer from his friends and generous applause from the enemy. After that Claflin tried a forward pass and gained another down, and then, from near the middle of the field, marched down to Brimfield's thirty-three before she was stopped. The Maroon-and-Grey got the ball on downs by an inch or two only.

Brimfield tried the Claflin ends out pretty thoroughly and with Otis and Howard carrying, took back most of Claflin's gain. But a forward pass finally went to a Claflin end instead of Holt and the tables were suddenly turned. It was the Blue's ball on Brimfield's forty-six then, and Claflin opened her bag of tricks. Just how Cox got through the centre of the Brimfield line no one ever explained satisfactorily, but get through he did, and after he was through he romped past Otis and Rollins and raced straight for the goal. Carmine and Howard closed in on him and it was Carmine who brought him down at last on the twelve yards.

How Claflin shouted and triumphed then! The Blue came surging down the field to line up against the astounded enemy, determination written large on every countenance. A plunge at Gilbert gained a yard and was followed by a three-yard gain off Holt.

Then Claflin fumbled and recovered for a two-yard loss and, with eight to go on fourth down, decided that a goal from field was the best try. And, although Brimfield tried hard to get through to the nimble-footed Cox, and did smear the Blue's line pretty fairly, the ball went well and true across the bar, and the 0 on the score-board was changed to a 3!

CHAPTER XXVI
LEFT GUARD GILBERT

THAT finished the scoring in the third period. All that Claflin could do was to bring back Brimfield's punts and try desperately to find holes in the maroon-and-grey line that weren't there. Both teams were showing the effects of hard playing, and when the third quarter ended substitutes were hurried in from both benches. For Brimfield, McPhee relieved Carmine, Lee went in for Holt and Sturges for Crewe. Claflin put in a new right end, a fresh full-back and returned her original right guard to the line-up.

McPhee brought instructions from Coach Robey. Brimfield was to hold what she had and play the kicking game. If she got within the Blue's thirty-yard line she was to let Rollins try a drop-kick.

Rollins punted regularly on second down and just as regularly Claflin rushed until the fourth and then punted back. After five minutes of play, during which the ball went back and forth from one thirty-yard line to the other, it dawned on Claflin that she was making no progress. A new full-back trotted in and displayed his ability by sending the ball over McPhee's head on his first attempt. Fortunately, though, the punt, while long, was much too low, and McPhee had plenty of time to go after the pigskin, gather it in and run back a dozen yards before the Claflin ends reached him. But after that McPhee played further back and Rollins put still more power into his drives.

With almost ten minutes of the final period gone, Claflin, grown desperate, tried what forward passing would do. The first time, she lost the ball to Thayer, and Clint got ten yards before he was thrown, but the second attempt went better and Cox, who made the catch, ran across three white lines and only stopped when Edwards dragged him down from behind. Claflin got another first down by two plunges at the right of the opponent's line and a wide end-run. Then a penalty set her back fifteen yards and she had to punt after two ineffectual attempts at rushing. Otis got through for five yards and then Rollins punted again.

The head linesman announced five minutes to play. On the stands the spectators were beginning to depart. Claflin was back on her thirty-five yards, banging desperately at the maroon-and-grey line, desperately and a bit hopelessly. A forward pass was knocked down by Captain Edwards, an assault at the left of the Brimfield line was smeared badly, Cox tried the other end and was laid low for a loss. Claflin punted.

Howard, on a double pass, swept around the enemy's left for fifteen yards and then squirmed past tackle for six more. Rollins kicked to Claflin's ten and Edwards nailed the Blue's quarter before he could move. Brimfield cheered encouragingly. But Claflin, after getting four around Sturges, punted out of danger to Brimfield's forty-seven.

"Three minutes!" announced the timekeeper.

Otis got two at centre and Rollins again fell back to kick. The ball came to him low and he juggled it. Claflin poured through the right of the line, the ball bounded back from some upthrown arm and went dancing along the field. Blue players and maroon dashed after it. Hall almost had it, but was toppled aside by a Claflin man. Carmine dived for it and missed. Then Tim Otis and a Claflin forward dropped upon it simultaneously and struggled for its possession. Tim always maintained that he got more of it than his opponent, and got it first, but the referee awarded it to Claflin and dismayedly Brimfield gathered together and lined up only twenty yards from her goal!

"Two minutes, fellows!" shouted the Claflin quarter-back exultantly. "We've got time to do it! Come on now, come on! We can win it right now! All together, Claflin! We've got them on the run! They're all-in! They're ready to quit!"

The Claflin full-back faked a kick and circled around Lee's end for a six-yard gain. Then the Blue's right half plugged the line and got three more past Hall. It was one to go on third down. Another attack on Hall was pushed back, but Claflin made it first down by sending Cox squirming around Thayer. The ball was on the eleven yards now. It was Brimfield's turn to know the fear of defeat. Edwards implored and bullied. Claflin banged at Gilbert for a yard. A quarter-back run caught Steve Edwards napping and put the pigskin on the seven yards. Brimfield's adherents, massed along the side line, shouted defiantly. Across the darkening, trampled field, the Claflin cohorts were imploring a touchdown.

"Third down! Six to go!" shouted the referee, hurrying out of the way.

"On side, Claflin right end and tackle!" warned the umpire.

The signals came again and the Claflin full-back smashed into the left of the opposing team. But it was like striking a stone wall that time. Perhaps the ball nestled a few inches nearer the goal, but no more than that. It was Don who bore the brunt of that attack and after the piled-up bodies had been pulled aside he and the Claflin full-back remained on the ground. On came the trainers with splashing buckets. Don came to with the first swash of the big, smelly sponge on his face. Danny Moore was grinning down at him.

"Are ye hurt?" he asked.

Don considered that a moment. Then he shook his head. "I'm—all right,—Danny," he murmured. "Just—help me—up."

"Don't be in a hurry. Take all the time the law allows ye." Danny's fingers travelled inquiringly over the boy's body. "Where do you feel it?" he asked.

Don kept his eyes stoically on the trainer's. If he flinched a little when Danny's strong fingers pressed his right shoulder it was so little that the trainer failed to see it. Nearby, the Claflin full-back was already on his feet. Tim came over and knelt by the trainer's side.

"Anything wrong, Don?" he asked in a tired, anxious voice.

"Not a thing," replied Don cheerfully. "Give me a hand, will you? I'm sort of wabbly, I guess."

On the side line Pryme, head-guard in hand, was trotting up and down. Coach Robey was looking across intently. Don shook himself, stretched his arms—no one ever knew what that cost him!—and trotted around a few steps. Then, out of the corner of his eyes, he saw the coach say something to Pryme, saw the disappointed look on the substitute's face and was half sorry for him. The whistle blew again and Don was crouching once more beside Thursby—why, no, it wasn't Thursby any longer! It was Peters, stout, complacent Peters, wearing a strangely fierce and ugly look on his round countenance!

"Now hold 'em, Brimfield!" chanted McPhee. "Hold 'em hard! Don't let them have an inch!"

Far easier said than done, though! A quick throw across the end of the line, a wild scramble and jumble of arms, a faint "Down!" and, at the right end of the Brimfield line, a mound of bodies with the ball somewhere down beneath and to all appearances across the goal line! Anxious moments then! One by one the fallen warriors were pulled to their feet while into the pile dove the referee. The timekeeper hovered nearby, watch in hand. Then the referee's voice:

"Claflin's ball! First down! A foot to go!"

"Line-up! Line-up!" shrieked the Claflin quarter. "We've got time yet! Put it over!"

"Fight, Brimfield!" shouted Steve Edwards. "There's only forty seconds! Hold them off! Don't let them get it! Tom! Peters! Don! Get into it now!"

"Signals! Signals!"

Then a moment of silence save for the gasping breath of the players. The Claflin quarter shouted his signals, the ball sped back, the lines heaved. Straight at the left guard position plunged the back. "Stop him!" growled Peters. The secondary defence leaped to the rescue. Back went the man with the ball. "Down!" he cried in smothered tones. The referee pushed in and heeled the mark.

"Second down! A foot and a half to go!"

Don knew now that if he had fooled Danny Moore he had not fooled the Claflin quarter-back. That quarter knew or guessed that he had been hurt and was playing for him. Don gritted his teeth and ground his cleats into the sod. Well, they'd see!

The signals again, broken into by Steve Edwards's shrill voice in wild appeal. Steve was wellnigh beside himself now. Peters was growling like a bear in a cage. Then again the plunge, hard and quick, the whole Claflin backfield behind it! Don felt an intolerable pain as he pushed and struggled. Despair seized him for an instant, for he was being borne back. Then someone hurtled into him from behind, driving the breath from his lungs, and he was staggering forward.

Peters was yanking him to his feet, a wild-eyed Peters mouthing strange exultant words. "They can't do it! No, never! Not if they were to try all night! We put 'em back again, Gilbert! We'll do it again! Come on, you blue-legged babies! Try it again! You'll never do it!"

Don, dazed, swaying giddily, groped back to his place. Thayer was muttering, too, now. Don wondered if they were all crazy. He was quite certain that he was, for otherwise things wouldn't revolve around him in such funny long sweeps. Then his mind was suddenly clear again. The Claflin quarter was hurling his signals out hurriedly, despairingly, fighting against time. Don didn't listen to those signals for he knew where the attack would come. And he was right, for once more the blue right guard and tackle sprang at him to bear him back. And then the runner smashed into sight, wild-faced for an instant before he put his head down and charged in. But Don didn't yield. Peters, roaring loudly, was fighting across him, and, front and rear, reinforcements hurled themselves into the mêlée. Don closed his eyes, every muscle in his body straining forward. A roar of voices came to him only dimly. Ages passed.

* * *

He wondered if Danny Moore had nothing better to do than eternally swab his face with that beastly old sponge! Why didn't he pick on some other fellow? Don felt quite aggrieved and tried to say so, but couldn't seem to make any sound. Then he realised that he had forgotten to open his lips. When he did he got a lot of cold water in his mouth and that made him quite peevish. He tried to raise his right hand, changed his mind about it and raised his left instead. With that he pushed weakly at the offending sponge.

"Take it away," he muttered. "I'm—drowned."

"Can you walk or will we carry you?" asked Danny in businesslike tones.

"Walk," said Don indignantly. "Let me up." Recollection returned. "Did they make it?" he gasped.

"They did not. Lie still a bit."

"Yes, but——" Don's voice grew faint and he closed his eyes again. The sponge gave a final pat and disappeared. "What—what down was that?" asked Don anxiously.

"Third."

"Then—then they've got another! Help me up, Danny, will you? We've got to stop them, you know. I don't believe they—can do it, do you? We put them back twice, you know."

"Sure you did," said the trainer soothingly. "Here you are, Tim. Take his feet. And you get your arm under his middle, Martin. So! Careful of the shoulder, boys. He's got a fine broken blade in there!"

"Wait!" Don kicked Tim's hands away from his ankles as, raised to a sitting posture by Danny and Martin, his puzzled glance swept the field. "Where's—where's everyone?" he gasped.

"If you mean the team," laughed Tim, "they're beating it for the gym."

"Oh!" said Don. "But—but what happened? They didn't"—his voice sank—"they didn't do it, did they, Tim?"

"Of course they didn't, old man! We pushed them back three times and we'd have done it again if the whistle hadn't saved them!"

"Then we won!" exclaimed Don.

"Surest thing you know, dearie! If you don't believe it listen to

142

that band of wild Indians over in front of the gym! Now are you ready to be lugged along?"

"Yes, thanks," sighed Don.

THE END